Forbidden Among the Stars

A Spicy Forbidden Age-gap Romance

Gwendolyn Morgan

Forbidden Among the Stars

A Spicy forbidden romance

ISBN #979-8-9901332-7-3

Contents

Author Notes

The author prohibits any entity from using any part of this publication—including text, cover, and internal graphics—for the purpose of training AI technology in any way. No part of this book may be reproduced in any form or by any electronic or mechanical means, including information storage and retrieval systems, without written permission from the author, except for the use of brief quotations in a book review. The author prohibits any entity from screening or running any part of this publication—including text, cover, and internal graphics—through any model proclaiming to be AI detection software without permission from the author. This book is sold subject to the condition that it shall not—by way of trade or otherwise—be lent, duplicated, sold, hired out, or circulated without the author's prior written consent. This includes any form of binding or other cover with which it is published. All images used have been obtained with appropriate copyright or licensing by those involved in the production.

Trigger Warnings

This is a forbidden romance book. It is a Reverse harem, so there is no choosing for the female main character. It had mature themes, including open–door romantic scenes, violence, coarse language, trauma, off–page, and talk of an unaliving (off page) This book is for ages 18+. If any of the themes have triggered you in the past, or you think you might be triggered by reading this story, then this book is not for you. Your mental health is more important than any story.

Gwendolyn

Also By Gwendolyn Morgan

The Divine Outcast Series

Book 1 - Prince of Shadows

Book 2 - Son of Storms

Book 3 - Born of Lightning

Book 4 - Daughter of War

The Crowned in Bloodlines Series

Book 1- Crowned in Rubies and Ruin

Book 2 - Crowned in Diamonds and Deception

Book 3 - Crowned in Sapphires and Seduction

Book 4 - Crowned in Emeralds and Ecstasy

The Divine Enchantment Series

Tangled in Deception

Embers of Revenge

The Soulbound Duet

King of Souls

Queen of Dusk and Dawn

Stand Alone Stories

Knaves of Her Heart

Forbidden Among the Stars

Orion

The city lights spilled across the floor-to-ceiling windows of Atlas' condo, reflecting off the polished marble like distant stars. Aries, Leo, and I walked through the sitting room and into the kitchen, the air thick with tension. Maeve on one side, Atlas on the other, and Andee in the middle. I could tell Andee was overwhelmed before she saw us walk in. Her face lit up as she leapt off the stool and hugged each of us.

"You came!" She said excitedly.

"Of course we did," Aries said with a cocky smile.

"Like we'd miss your high school graduation party, Andee," Aries added as she stood on her tiptoes to hug him.

"Everything okay in here?" I asked, looking at Maeve.

Her lips thinned. "Yes, Orion, everything's fine." Her words were terse as she looked at Atlas.

Atlas' eyes softened when Maeve started coughing. She put her hand up to let him know she was alright. Maeve had pneumonia a few weeks before, and it was holding on. Andee's face showed how worried she was. But Maeve distracted her with her world–famous spinach puffs, Andee's favorite.

Andee moved to the other side of the room and hugged her mum. Watching her get excited over something as simple as spinach puffs made me smile. Andee put them onto a serving plate and scooched past Leo, smacking at his hand as he tried to swipe one.

"Hey! These are for the guests!" Andee shrieked.

"Hey! We're guests!" Leo said with a pout.

Andee shook her head. "No, your family. You get the ones that didn't 'puff,'" she said, using air quotes with her free hand as she practically danced into the sitting room.

"Little brat," Leo mumbled under his breath. He was totally teasing; she loved to get after us, and we loved to egg her on.

Atlas looked at Maeve, who blew out a breath as Leo swiped a not so puffed up puff.

"Fuck, that's hot!"

I rolled my eyes. "No shit, Sherlock."

"Fuck off," he hissed, tossing another into his mouth.

I rolled my eyes again. "Whatever."

"Are you certain everything's good in here?" Aries asked, looking between Maeve and Atlas.

"Fine," Maeve said tightly.

Atlas let out a huff and stalked out of the room.

"Maeve, what's going on?" I asked.

"There's a reason I divorced him, Orion," Maeve bit out. "He's impossible!" She literally growled out her words.

"The college thing again?"

"What else?" She tossed the baking sheet into the sink, and the metal against metal sound made me wince.

"We'll talk to him," Leo assured her.

She balked, "Good luck. He's been acting strange again," she said, lowering her voice.

The three of us shared a look.

"We'll handle it."

"Thank you," Maeve said, turning back to make more food for the horde of eighteen-year-olds in the sitting room. The music made the entire condo shake so much that I felt it in my bones. It was too fucking loud, but I wasn't ready to be that guy yet. I refused. I was only thirty-five, but some days I felt more like sixty.

Andee was sitting on the edge of the sofa, legs crossed, her fingers fidgeting with the hem of her dress as Daphne, her best friend and another girl, were chatting up a storm, while Andee's eyes stared into nothing.

I knew what the fight was about, and I was pissed at Atlas for pushing. He wanted Andee to go to college in the city near him; Maeve, ever cautious, wanted to send her to a private one in the suburbs.

Atlas was on the balcony, the sky full of stars, the sounds of the city enveloping us. He didn't even look when the three of us joined him.

"She's impossible," he said, blowing out a breath. "She got to be part of Andee's life a lot longer than me. It's my turn."

"Did either of you ask Andee what she wanted to do?" Leo asked.

Atlas winced.

"Of course not," Leo bit out.

"She's not a little girl anymore," Aries said.

Atlas' eyes snapped to our friend's face. "She's not an adult either," he spat.

"Legally, she is," Aries hit back.

"She's too trusting, too vulnerable. I had to scare off her prom date. The asshole tried to take advantage of her."

I felt a growl leave my chest, which surprised even me. "You never said anything about that."

Atlas looked at me. "I handled it, Orion. She's not your responsibility."

"We've always watched out for her," Aries insisted.

Atlas shook his head. "And I appreciate it. But I've relied on you all too much."

"We would have done it even if you hadn't asked," Leo said, clapping him on the shoulder.

Atlas lowered his head. "You're right, she's not a kid anymore. She needs to make this choice."

His phone dinged, and he swiped it out of his back pocket. I didn't mean to glance at it. But I was glad I did.

"What the fuck, Atlas?" I roared, pushing his shoulder. "The fucking Moretti's? We talked about this already!"

"Hey!" Atlas hissed, his eyes narrowed at me.

"Don't you dare act like a self-righteous prick!" I pointed my finger toward the door. "You think she's vulnerable now, Atlas?"

Leo's eyes narrowed. "We talked about this, man. We agreed. I don't give a fuck about our safety, but Andee, it's a nonstarter, and you should know that. You're her father, for Christ's sake!"

Aries stepped away, looking like he was about to throw Atlas off the fucking balcony. His eyes narrowed at Atlas. "I'm going to see if Maeve needs help."

"What's his problem?" Atlas scoffed.

"What's his problem, Atlas? What the fuck do you think his problem is? You talking to the fucking mafia behind our backs!"

"For a second fucking time," Leo added with a rumble, stepping closer to Atlas.

Leo stepped aside, and I poked my finger at Atlas' chest, my voice low and cold. "Leave it the fuck alone, Atlas. No good will come of this. There's too much at stake."

We turned and stalked away before Atlas could argue.

My eyes flicked to Andee. She was biting her lower lip, nervous, uncertain. Every instinct screamed at me to pull her out of there, take her away from her fucking jackass of a father. She wasn't a kid anymore. She was danger in a minidress, and I hated myself for thinking of her that way. If Atlas didn't knock his shit off, she'd be in danger, more than we'd seen since we'd been in the service together.

The urge to protect her burned in me hotter than any star in the night sky. She was untouchable; her throaty laugh when she joked with us made restraint nearly impossible. She had to go to college away from all of this, not just to keep out of the danger her father might put her in, but from me. The most dangerous one of all.

Andee

Three years later

I stood stiffly in my crisp black dress; the morning sun was hitting me just enough to make sweat drip down my back. It was ninety degrees; the breeze barely a whisper, not helping in the slightest. I had chosen the same dress for my mother's funeral a little over a year ago. Now, there I was, wearing it again. This time, standing in front of my father's grave.

My mother knew she was dying. She didn't tell us until it was too late, but at least I could mentally prepare for it. This one felt unreal, a blur of sympathetic faces and whispered condolences, none of which could fill the hollow ache inside me. My heart was already shattered by my mother's death.

So much happened in the past year, I felt like I was drowning. A week before my mother died, my boyfriend, Matteo, came to my dad's condo. I thought he was there to help me through things. But he pulled me out onto the balcony and proposed instead. I was speechless. He was acting strangely, and I told him to leave several times; finally, my dad kicked him out. I'd never seen Matteo's eyes as cold as they were when he looked at my dad. But he left. Thank God. I broke off our two-year relationship because I didn't need that in my life. And if that wasn't bad enough, I was being harassed by my boss about all the time I was taking off. We were having drinks one night and Daphne and threatened to sue his ass, and after I stopped laughing, I convinced her I was alright and I could handle him.

The following morning, I told him I was going to HR, and his eyes narrowed, but he stopped. I was still working through my mom's death; and then Dad died. One of my dad's three business partners, Leo, broke the news to me.

I felt their presence behind me. Standing at my back like three silent sentinels, like they were my protection detail or something.

Orion Kane, Leo Sinclair, and Aries Thorne. Gods on Earth, sculpted like they'd been carved from marble and set loose into the world, but each carrying the weight of danger like it were nothing. All of them were around the same age as my father, all untouchable. Orion, with his sharp, calculating gaze, dark hair with the faintest hint of silver at his temples, was always three steps ahead, the strategist of the group. He runs the intelligence side of the company like a chess grandmaster, never missing a detail, always predicting moves before they happen. Ares, dark and untamed, muscles like coiled steel, tattoos crawling across his skin like warnings. He is the enforcer, the one who makes sure no one ever dared step too close in the field or outside it. And Leo, with his amber eyes, blond hair, and jaw that could cut glass, is the public face of the company, the negotiator, the one who can charm a room into submission while keeping his fists and mind ready if necessary.

They aren't just brilliant; they're dangerous. All former MI6 operatives, trained to anticipate, infiltrate, and eliminate threats before they ever become threats. And yes, all of them had British accents that wrapped around you like the devil himself, ruining the panties of hundreds of women, including me.

My father, Atlas Voss, convinced them to put their skills into forming Centari Security Group, a company that was so formidable that even the shadows hesitated to cross them. Their client list was more secure than all the gold in Fort Knox. I had no idea who they represented or what they did; all I knew was from little bits and pieces Daphne gathered from what she heard through closed doors at her father's law office. The one thing I knew for certain: they were all playboys. Each of them with a different woman on their arm at every gala and function in the city.

I hated how much I felt about them. They were all powerful and commanding. But standing here, my best friend holding my hand, I felt their eyes on me from where they were standing. Daphne squeezed my hand and her lips tipped so slightly no one else noticed. I turned my head slightly and caught Orion's gaze lingering, the heat of Ares' presence making my skin tighten, the smooth, intoxicating charm of Leo's smile that made me dizzy. I wasn't supposed to feel any of that; they were my father's partners, his best friends, men who watched me grow up.

Every time I thought about them, my mind drifted to the night of my twenty-first birthday. The night I drank way too much and went way too far with all three of them. If my father hadn't walked in, fuck only knows what would have happened. They ruined me for other men. After that night, I avoided them all. It was easy to forget about them that way, or at least that's what I told myself when just a week later, they all had new women on their arms at the latest gala. I didn't own them, and it was stupid to even think like that. It killed me to stay away. Each day the desire to hang out with them like we used to kept pulling at me. I told myself I could handle it. I was an adult. I could control my thoughts and desires.

And yet, as my gaze lingered on the three of them as they moved toward me, I realized I'd already lost control.

Orion

I stood a few paces back, shoulders squared, eyes never leaving her. Andee looked impossibly small in black. One hand clutching the folded handkerchief Aries gave her, and the other holding her best friend's hand as if it were the only thing keeping her grounded. The wind caught her hair; it was the first relief we'd gotten from the incessant heat that refused to let go, even though it was September and the leaves had begun to turn. Her golden waves scattered across her face, and for a moment, I forgot everything except her. Every quiet inhale she took made my chest tighten. It reminded me of the sound of her throaty laugh when she joked with Daphne at her twenty-first birthday party.

The sound that went straight to my cock. The unspoken desire for her haunted me longer than I cared to admit. I hated I wanted her. It was wrong. Not only was she young enough to be my daughter, she called me Uncle Orion for Christ's sake. At her twenty–first birthday, well, things almost got out of control, but she pulled away. It killed me, but it had to happen. I told myself the same thing since she was eighteen, and I thought I had it under control. She wasn't mine, and I had to wrap my head around that.

Andee's father Atlas was two years ahead of me in school, and Aries and Leo were two years behind me. But our parents were friends, and we hung out together for almost our entire lives. Atlas met Maeve, Andee's mum, while she was an exchange student, and the two fell for each other. They were only nineteen when Maeve had Andee. They got married, and Atlas got a job at a security company in London. He was a tech savant and the best negotiator in the business. We tried to convince him to join MI6 like the rest of us, but he didn't want to leave Maeve. But eventually, he convinced us that we should open our own security company.

We started Centari Security Group over a decade ago in a ten by ten rented office space, four desks practically on top of one another, taking the most demeaning security jobs imaginable. Then, Maeve's mum got sick, so she took Andee with her to the States. After a few years, the strain on their marriage was too much. They separated, and he sat us down and told us he couldn't put Andee through eight hour plane trips for visitation, so we moved the business. That's when it took off. And Atlas never let us forget it.

Andee carried herself like she already knew she was standing against shadows she couldn't see. But she was ours to protect now. And that would have to be the extent of it. Anything else would be beyond wrong. And yet, the way her blue eyes met mine, then flicked between Aries and Leo, then back to me, fuck if I didn't want to forget my morals, forget what society would think and make her ours.

My thoughts drifted to Atlas, and the anger hit harder than the grief. Not for the company. Not for what he left behind. For her. He knew what he was doing long before any of us did. Made choices he never explained, set things in motion he didn't trust us enough to stop. And in the middle of it all, he left her exposed. Even with the safeguards, even with us... it wasn't enough.

He was a bastard for that.

Whichever mafia organization he was working with put pressure on us, and Andee. But we weren't just men behind screens; we built security for people and governments that couldn't afford failure, and we did it without leaving a trace. MI6 taught us that control doesn't come from noise; it comes from precision, and most people would never understand what can be done from a keyboard when you know exactly where to look. We don't work with the mafia because our job is to prevent what they create. But if something threatens what we protect; we handle it just as ruthlessly.

I caught anomalies in the past couple of weeks: small security cameras hidden in vents, and the faint but persistent GPS ping from her car. It was more than worrisome. It was terrifying. With all our technology, the best on the fucking planet, we were still no closer to figuring out who was watching her. So we did the thing we knew best: we put cameras in her apartment, at the front of her building, and at her office. We even put an anti-tracking device in her car. She had no idea, and if she found out, all three of us knew the little firecracker would call us overprotective Neanderthals.

My number one priority was keeping Andee safe. I'd burn the entire fucking world for her if I had to.

Aries

I hated myself for the way my stomach clenched whenever Andee laughed. She was supposed to be untouchable and untangled from the dark world my partners, the men I considered brothers, and I navigated. Yet she'd invaded every corner of my thoughts. Every nerve screamed that it was wrong to want her, wrong to imaging her skin beneath my fingers, wrong to fantasize about her when all I should do was protect her. I protected her from the shadows her father ignored, all while wanting to pull her close, hold her tightly, and never let her go.

We didn't know who killed Atlas, the fourth in our brotherhood, but we knew he had gotten himself involved with the Mafia. We protect some of the most powerful and dangerous clients in the world, but that was one group we swore we'd never entangle ourselves with. We had been asked many, many times to do work for them. Orion, Leo and I had always been firm. Atlas, however, had slipped more than once.

He and Maeve had been divorced for almost ten years, and when he got the news she was sick, Atlas changed; obsessed, secretive, relentless. And although we owned one of the most advanced surveillance firms in the world, the man who helped build it knew exactly how to stay invisible. He was beyond devastated and got reckless, like he had nothing to lose. His only thoughts were making Maeve's pain go away. He stopped thinking about us and the business. None of us cared about our own safety, and the business was secure.

We confronted him about putting Andee in danger, and he swore he would end talks.

We thought he'd change back to the man we all knew since we were kids. We confronted him when Orion caught some anomalies in one of our systems. Again, he promised he'd stop, but he didn't, and three weeks later, was found in the park, with a gun in his hand and a suicide note. It was all fake, staged to make the police believe he had taken his own life. But it was a hit. And finding out who put out the hit was proving to be impossible.

To figure it out, I ran scenarios the way we were trained. Entry points, cameras, blind angles, human error. We refused to change our lives because of men who hide behind attacks like that. But Andee was the variable we couldn't factor. Even at ten, she was beyond precocious; she inherited Atlas' genius. I watched it for myself one afternoon. From the doorway, she could barely reach the desk, but she was already causing more headaches than a boardroom full of executives. She was kneeling on Atlas' desk chair, fingers flying across the keys with a confidence that should have been impossible for a kid her age. It was like slow motion, her finger hovering above one of the keys-when I called out to her.

"Andee, don't.."-I started, but she looked up at me with those wide, mischievous eyes, the corners of her mouth twitching. She hadn't broken anything *yet*. She watched me watching her as she smiled wide and pressed the button. The next thing I heard was Atlas cursing, and he ran into the room; the front of his pants was soaked. I tried not to laugh, but it was useless. I turned my head so Andee couldn't see me, but a laugh burst out anyway.

Atlas' face was one of exasperation and pride.

"Something the matter?" I asked, trying not to burst out laughing again.

Atlas looked at me, brows furrowed.

"Someone rerouted one of the minor protocols, causing the automation in the coffee machine to spew coffee all over the floor, and I was standing in the crossfire."

He turned to look at his daughter, who had slipped off his desk chair, looking up at him with her innocent doe eyes. "You wouldn't know anything about that, would you, Andromeda?"

She gulped at the use of her full name, but her golden curls shook around her. "I...I just wanted to see if I could," she said, as innocent as the day was long. Her arms were behind her back, and she was rocking back and forth on her toes. Atlas just shook his head and turned to leave the room to change. She looked extremely proud of herself, hopping back up on the chair and reversing what she had done in less than thirty seconds.

I knew then that she had inherited her father's mind. And that was something that could cause her to be in even more danger. And the thought of her in danger now ignited something primal. We would not fail. Not now, not ever. And yes, the guilt and the desire coiled together in a tense knot, but it only made me more feral, more determined. If anyone came for her, we would find them first.

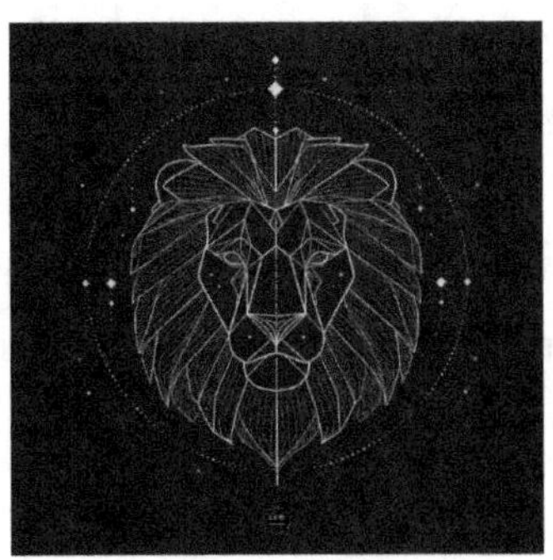

Leo

My chest tightened when Daphne hugged Andee. Andee was being the strong one, as always. She had always been smart, capable, but untested in the darkness our world demanded, and yet she carried herself with a stubborn pride that made me ache. She had a bratty little mouth for defying and teasing around with us, which over the past few years had become a more dangerous game to play. Because where it used to be innocent fun, the look in her eyes had changed when she pushed; she wanted a different response, and fuck if we all didn't want to give it to her.

It was fucked up, and I knew it, to watch her, to think about her the way I had was wrong, but irresistible. The temptation to cross the line became a gnawing need inside me. I tried to suppress it, finding other women to fuck, hoping to get the thoughts of her out of my system, was failing. No matter who I was with, it was Andee I was imagining moaning around my cock, screaming my name as she came apart under me. None of them sated the beast inside me. And I was disgusted with myself.

After the funeral, Orion put Andee in our company car; he walked over to where Aries and I were standing. His eyebrows pinched as he handed me a small black book.

"Andee found this in with Atlas' things. It's all ciphers and codes that we'll have to put through the software," Orion rasped. "It's not the only one," he said with a frustrated sigh. "Apparently there are nearly twenty at the condo."

I let out a hiss. "Fuck."

Orion nodded. "Tell me about it."

"Feels a lot like we're going to be opening a Pandora's box of questions," Aries said with a huff of a laugh.

"Once the reading is over, we need to decide what we're going to do," Orion said.

I quirked a brow. "What we're going to do?"

"About her," he said, looking toward the car.

"We've done all we can," I said. "Her building, car, phone, office, and everywhere she shops, eats, and visits have the latest surveillance tech. Cost us a fortune, but she's worth it."

"He's left his quarter to her," Aries said.

We looked at him. "Robert hinted at it at the church," he added.

Orion stroked his chin. "It's not surprising. But it makes things more complicated."

"She needs to know, make her own decision on what to do. Selling it to us would be the best. Then she'd be free and clear," I said.

"Would she?" Aries asked. "We have no idea what Atlas was doing. We have three mafia families under surveillance, and still don't know which one he was talking to."

The entire situation was dangerous, from whatever angle you looked at it, but our determination about her safety never would waver.

We were at Atlas' condo in the city. The reading went as expected. Andee got an equal stake in the company. Now we just had to convince her that selling it to us was the best for her, and pray that she didn't get stubborn like she usually did. Still, we didn't want to overwhelm her; selling her share needed to be addressed, and the rest could be talked out later.

"Hey kiddo," I said, walking into the kitchen. I stopped dead in my tracks. She was bent over the dishwasher. Her perfect little ass barely covered by her tiny black dress. If she had bent over further, I'd have seen...fuck.

"Oh, hey Leo," she said with her sunny smile that made my heart squeeze as she turned to face me. Aries and Orion joined us.

Her face fell. "What's going on?"

Aries shook his head. "Nothing bad, sweets, I promise," he smiled.

"Is this about the shares?"

I nodded. "Yes. We wanted to talk to you about them. How do you feel about it?"

Aries looked at me, so did Orion. That wasn't something we had talked about asking her, but I felt it was the right thing to do.

"I'm not sure," she said, twisting the towel between her hands so tightly her knuckles turned white. Orion reached for it.

"It's already dead, sweetheart, give it here," he chuckled.

She always was a fidgeter. Atlas pulled his hair out trying to get her to stop, but it never worked. She winced and handed the towel to Orion, and clasped her hands together behind her back to keep from fidgeting.

"So, the shares?" I asked, returning to the subject at hand.

"What do you think I should do?" She asked innocently, and fuck me, those lips.

Aries shook his head. "It's up to you, Andee. It's a lot of responsibility."

"Not that you can't handle it." I narrowed my eyes at him.

Andee laughed.

"What are my options?"

Orion cleared his throat. "Keep them, and learn the business, or sell them to us and go traveling like you've always dreamed of," he said, sweetening the pot. That was the option we all hoped she would go for.

Her eyes widened and her lips tipped up. "There would be enough for me to do that?" She was practically bouncing on her toes.

I laughed. "There would be enough for you to travel for the next sixty years, and have enough left over for your great-grandchildren."

Her jaw dropped. "Holy fuck."

Orion cocked an eyebrow. "Language."

She put her hand on her hip. "I'm not a kid anymore, *Uncle Orion,*"

I stifled a rumble. Her lip was pouted, and all I wanted to do was bite it. It didn't get past me that Orion stepped behind the kitchen Island and Aries walked the opposite direction to get himself a bottle of water.

But then Orion stepped toward her, his eyes full of promise. "You may be all grown, little one, but I can still punish you."

What the fuck?

Andee's eyes widened, and a blush crept up her neck. She nearly tripped over her own feet as she dashed out of the kitchen.

"What the fuck was that?" I growled, punching Orion in the arm.

"I..fuck..."-Orion stammered, scrubbing his hand down his face.

"Yeah, I'd say," I scoffed.

"That was stupid. So very stupid," Aries said, shaking his head slowly.

"Okay, Mr. Walk away because of the tent in my slacks," Orion lobbed back.

Aries rolled his eyes. "Cause you didn't make anything obvious by moving behind the island."

"Would you two shut the hell up?" I roared. I turned to Orion. "Fix it," I growled.

He let out a breath and nodded.

I hate to admit, if it hadn't been him, it would have been me. And fuck I hated myself for it.

Andee

Orion stepped toward me, his eyes full of promise. *"You may be all grown, little one, but I can still punish you."*

Holy mother of God.

I didn't walk out of the kitchen; I ran. My cheeks were hot and my panties were wet; the ache between my thighs was like nothing I'd ever experienced before. And all because of one sentence from the man I'd been lusting after. I could have played it cool, teased back, but no, I ran like a scared little rabbit.

"They're really going to think you're mature now, dummy," I hissed at myself as I closed the door to the room I used at my dad's condo. I now owned a fourth of his company. I wasn't stupid, I knew how the guys all lived, the cars they drove, the properties and yachts, all of it, I had no idea a fourth of the company would be worth enough to travel for the better part of my life, and have money left over. I guess I never thought too much about it.

I picked up my phone and video called Daphne.

"Hey love, what's up?" She asked cheerfully.

I told her about my new reality, and she beamed.

When she gave me a sly smile, I cocked my eyebrow. "You knew, didn't you?"

She smiled. "Maybe," she laughed. "I'm not at liberty to say," she teased.

I waved her away with my hand and told her about Orion.

"Holy mother of God!"

"That's what I said!"

"What did you do?"

"What do you think? I got the fuck out of there like the scared little rabbit I am."

She laughed. "It's okay, you know."

"What's okay?"

"To want to fuck them all," she smiled, then laughed.

"Oh my god!" I felt my cheeks warm. "Can we please stop talking about my dad's best friends, the men who I call my uncles?"

She gave me a devious smile. "By the blush on your cheeks right now, I would have to call you a liar with daddy issues."

"Eww. Stop! Oh my god! I'm hanging up now!"

She laughed so hard I couldn't help it; I started laughing too. After we both caught our breath, her voice turned more serious.

"You should take the deal," she said. "You've wanted to travel since we were kids, and you had to give that up when your mom got sick. It's time you put yourself first, Andee."

"I don't know," I said, nibbling at my lip.

"Tell them you want to sell, then tell your landlord you're traveling for the next sixty years, so you're moving out, and then tell your asshole boss to fuck himself, or I'll do it for you."

I laughed at my best friend. But she wasn't kidding. She would do all those things.

"I love you, you know that?"

"Obviously," she chuckled. "Now, you need to call my cousin and make travel plans for at least the next six months, understand?"

I mock saluted.

"Oh, and Andee?"

"Yeah,"

"Go crazy for one night."

"Um, no."

"Chicken."

I laughed. "Bwak, bwak."

"Love you."

"Back at you," I said, ending the call.

There was a knock at the door. "Andee, can I come in?" Orion's deep voice flowed through the door, and suddenly I couldn't breathe.

"Yeah," I said, trying not to sound like a dumb teenager.

He opened the door and strode into the room, closing the door behind him.

Despite my best efforts, my breath shuttered. Actually shuttered. And the look in his eyes told me he had noticed. But he schooled his face and sat on the chair across from me.

He ran his hand through his dark hair. "About earlier... I.."

I waved my hand, shaking my head. "We don't have to talk about it, Orion." I hated the vulnerability in my voice.

"It was inappropriate. I don't know what came over me. I'm sorry."

"Already forgotten," I said with a smile.

Liar.

He let out a breath. "Thank you," he said, as he rose from the chair, turning to leave.

"Orion?"

"Yes, Andee?"

"I want to travel. I'll sell."

His face was unreadable, but then he smiled. But it didn't reach his eyes.

"Wonderful, I'll tell the others. Start planning your travel."

I smiled. "Thanks."

The following morning, I ran into the coffee shop on the corner, and who was walking out? Matteo, of course. Like a dummy, I agreed to have a cup of coffee with him. He laid it on thick, and I didn't say no. Big mistake.

"You look good, Andee," Matteo said easily, studying me in that way that always felt like he saw more than he should.

I sat, forcing a polite smile. "Thanks. You too."

We talked about nothing at first, safe things, surface things, mutual friends, his family, the way people do when they're pretending something isn't broken.

For a moment, I almost relaxed.

Until he leaned back in his chair, eyes settling on me in a way that made my stomach tighten.

"I've been patient," he said casually.

My fingers stilled around my glass. "About what?"

"You," he replied, like it were obvious. "About you coming to your senses."

The air shifted.

"It's been over a year, Matteo. That's not going to happen."

Matteo didn't react the way I expected. No anger. No frustration. Just that same calm.

He smiled, but it didn't reach his eyes. "You say that," he murmured. "But you've always known how this ends."

He tried to touch my hand; I pulled it away, my chest tightened, and I shook my head.

His eyes narrowed. "Is this because of *them?*"

"Who?"

He almost laughed. "The men. The ones who always look at you like they want to fuck your brains out."

I didn't know how to respond. My heart raced.

"It is, isn't it? Don't lie to me."

"I'm not. They are my dad's business partners, nothing more."

Something flickered in his expression, not anger. Something colder. He studied my face, like he didn't believe me.

"I thought I told you not to lie to me," he said with venom in his tone.

"I'm not," I hissed. I was about to walk out. I was pissed. He was crazy. Hadn't spoken to me in a year, and yet, there he was, acting like a fucking Neanderthal.

That's when I saw him. Aries, walking into the coffee shop. Matteo's eyes narrowed. He looked like an unhinged monster, and it terrified me. I shook my head, and his demeanor changed. Gone were his cold eyes, replaced by the respectful man he always was in front of them.

"Mr. Thorne, so nice to see you." Matteo's fake smile made a shiver run through me as he shook Aries' hand.

"Matteo," Aries said with no emotion in his tone.

Matteo swallowed his last gulp of coffee and rose from the table.

"Well, it was nice catching up, Andee. Safe travels."

My blood ran cold, and I felt the color drain from my face. How did he know?

Aries watched him walk out. "Are you okay?"

I shook myself out of my daze. "Yeah, just tired."

He raised a brow at me.

"I promise," I said, lighter.

He considered me, then smiled, offering a hand. "Need a ride home?" His smile made me suppress a shiver.

"Sure," I smiled back.

He offered his arm, and I laced mine through his as we left. But I felt eyes on me. Matteo was sitting in his car, watching.

I didn't tell Aries. I was too afraid, so I suppressed it and decided Matteo was fucking with me. He didn't know my plans; he couldn't. Could he?

Orion

I leaned against the wall next to Andee's room, gently banging my head against it. Fuck. She wanted to sell. It was the best option, but made my entire body feel like I'd been hit by a truck. I was an asshole. I wanted her to stay. As I walked into the sitting room, thoughts of how to convince her to stay swam through my mind.

I heard her on the phone with Daphne. Yes, I was listening. Yes, I heard Daphne tell Andee she had daddy issues, and Andee didn't deny it. And fuck me, I had to stand outside her room until my cock calmed the fuck down.

"She wants to sell," I told the others.

Aries looked up from his phone, and Leo looked from the window to me. Neither of them wanted her to choose that option either.

Aries said the thing we were all thinking. "We're a bunch of assholes, aren't we?"

I didn't have to say anything. We all knew it. Even after the night of her twenty-first birthday. The party was at Atlas' condo, full of twenty-one-year olds. A lot of eyes were on us, which wasn't good, but we avoided the stares and sultry glances from Andee's friends, choosing to hang out in Atlas' den instead. He mysteriously disappeared as the guests started thinning out, and once it was quiet in the other room, we went to help Andee clean up. But she wasn't cleaning up. She was drinking. A seven hundred dollar bottle of Atlas' best whisky.

The stress of Maeve dying a month earlier and her dad going on trips for weeks at a time, she was in an extremely vulnerable place. And we crossed a line. Big time.

"Andee, sweetheart, give me the bottle," I coxed, kneeling next to her.

She pulled it to her chest. "No, Orion, It hurts too much."

Leo sat next to her, brushing her golden hair out of her face. "What hurts too much, little one?"

"Mom being gone. I don't want to feel it anymore."

Aries sat on the other side of her and gently pulled the bottle away. Her head snapped toward him.

"What don't you want to feel, sweetheart?" Aries asked.

"The emptiness. I'm all alone."

I shook my head. "You're not alone; you've got Daphne, your dad, and us."

She shook her head. "Dad's gone all the time, Daphne is going to work at her dad's firm in Europe, and you guys are always busy with work, or women," she said with a little eye roll.

My lips twisted into a smile. "You know you can call us anytime for anything."

She didn't say anything for a minute; she just looked between the three of us.

"Let's get you to bed," Leo said, reaching for her hand.

"Wait!" She hiccuped. "You didn't give my birthday kiss. A sly smile arched her beautiful pink lips. "You always each give me a kiss on my birthday," she said in a tone that made my cock twitch. I was such an asshole.

A slow, almost imperceptible smirk tugged at the corners of Leo's lips. The bastard discreetly moved his shirt lower over his lap.

At least I won't be alone in hell, I thought to myself.

Even Aries looked like he was grappling with his own demons.

"Yes, Leo said with a calm and measured tone. "A kiss on the cheek." His hand hovered near hers, brushing her fingers so slightly. Goosebumps skated over her skin, and I actually hated that her body was responding to Leo and not me.

Andee's head turned. "Mmm," she purred softly, "but maybe I want more."

She was killing me. Leo stifled a groan, and Aries' eyes shifted, like a storm about to break.

The tension in the room thickened. Leo leaned back, arms crossed, a smirk playing on his lips, as he watched Andee and me.

"You're playing with fire, little one."

Her eyes glinted in the candlelight. "I like fire," she said, a sly smile crossing her lips as if to say, 'checkmate.'

A sharp chuckle escaped Leo, and Aries's grin widened, almost predatory. Both men's eyes flicked between her and me, the unspoken tension of wanting her impossible to ignore.

She leaned forward. Her scent of roses and rain made me rumble low in my chest.

"Andee," I warned.

She moved closer anyway, our lips inches from one another.

"It's my birthday, Orion, she whispered. "Just one. *Please?*"

One kiss, like it could ever be just that, but the tensioned snapped, my fingers brushed against her jaw, then my hand moved, almost against my will, as it grasped around her neck, and I pulled her toward me.

"You don't know what you're asking, little one," I rumbled against her ear.

Her head turned. "I think I do."

That was the moment I lost. My lips brushed hers, giving her time to stop me, to laugh it off, to save us both. She didn't. Her fingers curled into my shirt instead, anchoring me there. The kiss was gentle. Careful. A brush of our lips, more than anything else. But that's all it took.

Her breath caught against my lips, warmth sparking down my spine, years of restraint cracking in one quiet, devastating second. I felt every inch of the boundary breaking, the rules, the logic that had kept distance between us.

I pulled back first; the desire in her eyes nearly made me reach for her again. But she had already turned to Leo, grasping his shirt, pulling him toward her. He didn't stop her; their lips crashed against each other, a soft moan escaped her lips as his hand tangled in her hair. Aries' eyes were full of fire, a man under the spell of the woman in front of us. He reached for her arm, turned her toward him, and pulled her against his chest.

His kiss wasn't gentle; their tongues tangled, but the moment she moaned his name, the spell broke.

They broke apart like a rubber band snapping. Her lips were pink and puffy; she tried to catch her breath.

"I'm... *fuck.*" Her murmur broke me. Her cheeks turned a bright shade of pink.

"Andee..."– I stammered.

Then the door slammed open, making me jump as Atlas stepped into the room. The three of us surrounded his daughter in a way none of us had a right to be, and yet, there we were. His eyes narrowed. Andee pushed off the couch and bolted. Atlas' face had murderous intent. But he took a breath.

"Get the fuck out," he said. His calm voice rattled me more than his rage would have.

The three of us were silent on the way home. None of us wanted to face what we had done. I know if Atlas hadn't walked in, I wouldn't have stopped. Before he walked into the room, I was going to convince her it was okay to choose us, like an asshole.

Atlas didn't speak to us for weeks, and Andee avoided us like the plague, and it killed all of us. But it was better that way.

At least that's what I kept telling myself.

The morning after Andee's twenty-first birthday, we sat in the kitchen, each of us holding our heads like we had the worst hangovers in the world. I felt like the biggest asshole, and I know the others did as well. What we did was a mistake. Atlas' calm tone was scarier than when he was yelling, but to be honest, we deserved more than just his ire. I tossed and turned all night, my cock strained against my boxers, thinking of her.

I deserved to be in hell.

Aries walked in, shrugging off his jacket and plopping into one of the chairs. I watched him search on his phone with his brows knitted.

"What's up?" I asked, not looking away from my computer.

"I gave Andee a ride to her apartment," he said, as he continued to scroll on his phone.

"And?" Leo asked.

"And she was with her ex, Matteo."

"She was what?" I hissed.

Aries shook his head. "I don't think she wanted to be. I watched them through the window, and she was extremely tense until she saw me. Then he acted as if he actually respected me," he said with a half laugh.

"I never liked him," Leo rasped as he started typing furiously on his laptop. "Matteo DeLuca," twenty-two, and is a trust fund baby. His father is president of several banks. He's bounced around jobs over the past few years, mostly owned by his father."

We searched for over an hour; there were no other red flags that popped up about Matteo, yet I had a sinking feeling about him showing up after a year. We never knew why they broke up. I wanted to ask Andee, but with everything else going on, I didn't want to upset her. So we let it go.

"We need to keep track of him," Aries said.

"Agreed."

Leo

Sitting in the kitchen a few mornings after the funeral, Orion let out a breath, finally breaking the silence. "The security is set up at the little house she's renting in Amsterdam, and we have a few 'neighbors' that can keep us updated if anything suspicious happens."

I blew out a breath.

"It's the best. We can't keep her here. It's not fair to her," Orion admitted.

"I know we need to let her go," I said. Even though the words tasted like ash in my mouth.

Both of my friends nodded in agreement, even though no one wanted to.

Three weeks later

"I swear to fuck, if you hit that computer one more fucking time," Aries warned.

"It's a piece of shit!" I hissed.

"It's brand fucking new!" Aries bit back.

"It's taking forever with this algorithm!"

"It's been two minutes. Calm the fuck down!"

I literally growled at the computer. We'd been decoding Atlas' book for the past three weeks. We crashed at his condo, hoping we'd find more on his multiple servers and laptops. We were still trying to get his codes to make sense and if anything; they were more jumbled than when we started. None of us could think straight. Andee had her travel plans made; she quit her job within hours of the money from the share sale hitting her bank account. Not all of it, of course. Most of it was in an offshore account where she could access it, but it wouldn't raise any red flags or attract unwanted attention.

The awkwardness between all of us settled back in, and it was making me crazy. We'd been around her again for just a few days, and it was the most normal I felt in months, and here we were, back to not seeing her, and it was like I had the wind knocked out of me. I couldn't take a full breath. We tried to get her out of our system, and we were failing miserably. My last two dates were disasters. Aries all out refused, taking more cold showers in the past three weeks than in our entire time in the service. And Orion had just brought a date back to the condo. At our penthouse, we had a hard and fast rule: no women. We had plenty of other places we could bring them. Since this was the place we were spending most of our time, he brought her here and took her right upstairs to the bedroom we had re-furnished. We didn't touch Andee's room, but we turned Atlas's office into three more bedrooms.

After futzing with the fucking computer for another twenty minutes, a woman's voice rang down the stairs.

"And just who the *FUCK* is Andee?" She screamed.

"Oh, shit." Aries' smile was contagious, as we tried to ignore the blond woman screeching at Orion, who was lazily walking down the stairs behind her.

"There's a car waiting for you..."-

The woman turned, her eyes shooting daggers at him. "MELINDA! You jackass!" She screamed, turning on her heel and storming out.

Orion looked at us. "Not one word."

Aries laughed his ass off.

"Oh, it's way too late for that, brother," I hissed out in laughter.

He poured himself a drink and sank into the couch, leaning his head back.

"She's the model, right?" I asked with an air of teasing.

"Oh, who the fuck cares?" Orion hissed as he sipped his drink.

"This is getting ridiculous," I rasped.

"I told you. Let it process for Christ's sake!" Aries hissed.

"Not the computer you ass," I bit back.

"We agreed not to talk about it," Orion said, almost lazily.

"Fuck the agreement. She leaves in two days."

Orion raised a brow. "And?"

"And. None of us can think straight. The two women I've fucked make me feel like I'm with a robot. You can't keep her name out of the bedroom, and Aries has used more cold water in the past three weeks than sunk the fucking Titanic."

Aries shook his head. "We can't."

"Who says? Society? When the fuck have we ever cared about what the fuck society thinks about anything?"

Both men considered what I had said.

"If we do this. We make the rules crystal clear. For all of us," Orion said.

"And then we let her go," Aries added.

I nodded. "But not here, and not at the penthouse."

"Then where.." Orion started. My eyes sparkled, and he shook his head, "She'd never agree. Besides, we're pushing the boundary as it is."

"This is already off the fucking rails, and if we're doing this, I'm not holding back," I told them both.

"How do we get her there?"

"Leave that to me," I said, wiggling my brows.

Orion shook his head. "You scare me sometimes, you know that?"

I just beamed as I pressed a button on my phone and it rang on the other end.

Orion's Jeep pulled into the garage of the Velvet Underground, a speakeasy owned by a client of ours. A very expensive, exclusive club that catered to those who preferred to play with no one knowing their business. We set up the security for the place a few years ago. The owner, Sebastian Hale, was a friend from back home; we gave him the 'friends and family' discount, and he gave us VIP memberships for life.

I sent VIP passes to Daphne the day before, anonymously, of course. We knew Daphne was into this type of thing, and though Andee was kind of shy, we knew Daphne could talk her into almost anything. We had a little over twelve hours, and we planned on keeping our little firecracker until the very last minute. We cancelled her flight to Amsterdam, setting her up with one of our jets instead. We agreed to put her on the plane and send her off, all of us convinced that would be the end of it, and we could all get back to our lives. We knew Andee slept like death when she drank even a couple of glasses of wine, so we agreed that was the best way to get her on the plane while she was sleeping. We had one of our employees, Ben, go to her apartment and bring her luggage to the jet as soon as Daphne picked her up.

After about thirty minutes, we all turned our heads at the same time. Even through the mask she wore, we knew it was her. She wore a phoenix mask, and her eyes flicked around the room as Daphne handed her a drink.

I wasn't very subtle about my mask choice; I wore a gold lion mask. Aries and Orion opted for a wolf and a leopard, keeping on theme, because I had my predatory, possessive eyes on one specific little creature. I gently elbowed Orion.

His eyes widened. Then Aries noticed the band around her wrist. "Such a naughty little thing," he chuckled darkly. We waited until Andee had mostly finished her drink before we stalked our little prey. Daphne saw us first; her eyes widened, and she smiled, moving to the side and ordering another drink. Andee was watching everything going on around her, and she bit her bottom lip. We came around her, encircling her. Her breath hitched as Orion whispered in her ear.

"Hello little flame."

Aries

Andee's breath hitched, and her eyes flicked between the three of us.

"Arie.."-

Orion put his finger to her lips. "No names, little flame. One night, then you go your way, we go ours, understand?"

She nodded.

"I need your words, little flame," he rasped.

"Ye..yes.."-

"Good girl."

My cock swelled when she shivered at Orion's words. I took her hand, looking at the band on her wrist. "Interesting and bold choice, little flame," I murmured.

"It was Daphne's idea."

"You could have said no," Orion's deep voice enveloped her, and she shivered again. "Does the thought excite you?"

She didn't answer. Orion pulled her against him. "Answer me, little flame."

"Ye..yes."

"Good girl," he murmured against her neck.

Leo took her hand, and we walked down to the private rooms. He pushed the code to open the door, and it clicked. The room consisted of an enormous bed, a sitting area, a bar, and a fireplace, already crackling, giving the room a soft glow. An ensuite bathroom was on one side of the room. The three of us sat in chairs, and Orion pulled Andee onto his lap. Her eyes widened as she clearly felt his cock under her perfect little ass.

"Now, there are rules tonight, little flame," he rasped. "You belong to us tonight, all of you. You listen to what we tell you and be a good girl, or we will punish you and that bratty little mouth of yours." He swiped his thumb across her lower lip, and her tongue darted out. "Do you understand?"

"Yes."

"Yes, what?"

"Yes, Daddy."

Fuck me. I nearly came when she called Orion daddy.

Orion's eyes darkened. "Now, on your knees, and take out my cock."

She slid off his lap and unhooked his belt, unbuttoned his slacks, and Orion's hiss filled the room when she freed his cock. Both Leo and I freed our cocks, just watching her hand on his made mine ache. We had shared women, fucked them alone and together. By the time they left the room, their names were practically a distant memory. But tonight? Tonight would be seared into my brain for the rest of my life, whether I liked it or not.

She grasped Orion's cock and licked the pre-cum off the tip like she was licking an ice cream cone. Orion's hand tangled in her hair as he hissed out a curse.

"Such a good girl," he hissed as she took him further into her mouth. "Play with that little pussy of yours while you suck my cock."

Her right hand slid into her panties, and she moaned around Orion's cock as I slid to my knees, turned onto my back and slid between her sumptuous thighs. The sound of her lace panties ripping filled the air as she gasped. I flicked her little nub and her hips moved as I nipped at her clit, and her moans around Orion's cock made me pump my own with my other hand as I slowly fucked her with my tongue. Her little gasps were music to my ears.

"Do you like your pretty little pussy being eaten out, little flame?" Orion hissed as she mumbled around his cock.

"Such a good little girl for us," Leo said, his breath raspy as I heard his hand moving up and down on his cock. I flicked Andee's clit, and she moaned. I slowly went between fucking her deep and barely touching her clit with the tip of my tongue. Her thighs shook, and her moans floated through the air, and I sucked on her clit hard. Her muffled scream filled the air around Orion's cock.

"Oh my God! Fucckkk! "Yes!" Her pussy milked my tongue and I couldn't wait until it was my cock. I continued to fuck her through her orgasm and when she stopped shaking, I moved out from under her. She continued to suck on Orion's cock as he pressed her head down, praising her. His hips bucked and his roar filled the room as Andee swallowed every drop of his cum. Leo and I weren't far behind.

"Such a good girl," Orion praised. "Get on the bed."

"Yes, Daddy," she moaned as she moved to the bed. Leo slid her shoes off, and Orion sat her up, helping her out of her dress. She was like a banquet laid out before us. All three of us undressed, and she watched, licking her lips. Her hands slid down my abs as I hovered over her perfect breasts, flicking them with my tongue, her body arched.

"So responsive," Leo said, running his hand down her creamy thighs. "Spread those legs for me, baby girl. Show me that pretty little pussy."

Her legs opened and her glistening pussy was drawing me like a fly to honey. Leo licked her pussy, and she moaned.

"Fuck me, you taste good," he murmured against her. Her hand caught in his hair as she pulled him toward her so his tongue would go deeper. She fucked herself on his tongue as he flicked her nipples and she fisted the sheets. I moved toward her mouth, and her tongue flicked against my cock as she licked and sucked while Leo fucked her beautiful little cunt. Orion fisted his cock, moving her hand in place of his.

"I'm going to paint those beautiful tits with my cum," Orion hissed. She moaned around my cock and my hips jerked.

"Look at you," Orion praised. "Such a good girl," he hissed as her hand moved faster. She screamed around my cock as Leo sucked her clit, her entire body shuddering. I didn't last, not after watching her come for a second time. My release flowed down her throat as Orion's cum hit her perfect breasts and she climaxed again from Leo's tongue.

"Holy fuck," she breathed.

I watched Orion nearly call her out for her bratty mouth, but he didn't.

We cleaned her up, and Orion hovered over her.

"Are you on birth control, little girl?"

"Yes, Daddy," she murmured,

"Good," he growled. "Because I don't want anything between my cock and this pretty little cunt," he rasped as he thrust inside her.

"Oh, fuck!" She screamed as he grasped her hips and fucked her hard. Her tits bounced and Leo and I each took one into our mouths. She moaned and screamed as Orion continued his assault on her pussy.

"Such a tight little pussy," Orion hissed as she moaned his name.

He growled as he continued to fuck her, his eyes never leaving hers.

"I...Oh my god! Please don't stop! I need to come! Please let me come!"

Orion pinched her clit, and she exploded, her little body shaking as Leo and I continued to suck her nipples. Orion roared his release, and he kept inside her until she stopped shaking. He kissed her neck as I helped clean her up. After she settled, and I handed her a glass of wine, and Leo brought out a charcuterie board.

None of us talked. Though I wanted to, because I was having second thoughts. I could tell Orion and Leo were feeling the same as they watched her drink her wine and take bites of cheese and olives.

But then Orion's face shifted as he watched her. "That's a good girl. We need to keep your strength up. We have a long night ahead of us."

Andee

My entire life was packed. I stored some things at my dad's condo, purposely making sure the guys weren't around when I dropped my stuff off. I was avoiding them again. While it was super awkward being with them again, it was also comfortable and familiar. I had to push the thought of them aside. I was moving on with my life. It was the best thing for me, for all of us.

My phone rang, and Daphne practically screamed over the other end. "Oh my God! Guess where we're going tonight?"

"Um, nowhere. I leave at eleven AM tomorrow."

"Girl! You think I'm letting you stay home on your last night in town? Especially when I have two VIP invitations to the Velvet Underground? Not on your life!"

"The Velvet Underground? How did you get VIP invites?"

"Excuse me," Daphne balked. "I know people," she said, sounding extremely haughty. I laughed at my friend.

"I'm not so sure," I have more packing and.."-

"No more excuses. I'll be there at seven. I'm coming in to get you so you'd better be ready or I'll pick your outfit for you!"

"All my dresses are packed," I said with a snarky tone, though she knew I was teasing.

"I'll bring a dress and shoes!"

"Nothing too slut.."-

She hung up. The little shit. Daphne was about two inches shorter than I was. Making any dress she owned practically a tank top on me. The entire thing sounded fishy, and I told Daphne that several times on our way to the club.

I shivered as we entered the club, and a sultry brunette greeted us with a friendly smile. When Daphne slid the invitations toward the woman, her eyes nearly bugged out of her head. She schooled her face and handed us what looked like a menu.

I balked at the list. "So many things to choose from."

"I'll have the strawberries, extra cream, and she'll have the Aged Reserve Special." Daphne nearly snorted; she laughed so hard.

The woman looked at us as if she was going to revoke our passes, but she handed us bracelets. Red and white for Daphne, and amber for me.

The woman had us choose masks; Daphne picked a dove and handed me a red, gold, and orange phoenix mask.

"The rules are: no names, and do not remove your masks," the woman said.

"Understood," Daphne said.

I looked at my bracelet. "Anything you'd like to share with the class?" I asked as she looped her arm through mine.

"Nope," she giggled.

"I *so* don't believe you."

She winked at me as we walked into the main room of the club. All eyes were on us as I took in the room. The entire place smelled of perfume and sex. Every surface was covered in purple velvet, except for the small tables that dotted the room. The eyes of both men and women flicked to our wrists as we walked up to the smooth wooden bar and ordered two glasses of merlot. I watched several couples making out, and some groups of men and women, and some same-sex partners. One woman was getting eaten out by another woman while she sucked on a man's cock.

I felt my cheeks warm as I took a sip of my drink.

Daphne tapped my arm with her elbow. "Does anyone strike your fancy?"

I shook my head. "No, not yet."

"Well, it's still early," she smiled as a man wearing a tiger mask walked up to her.

"You leave me and I will kill you."

She smiled at the man. "Maybe later," she said in a sultry voice. He nodded once and turned, walking toward a group of women instead.

My drink was nearly gone when Daphne's eyes sparkled. She flashed a smile at someone across the room. She moved a few seats away from me.

"What are you.."-

The hair on my neck stood up when I felt not one, not two, but three hard bodies against my back. A shiver ran down my spine when one of them grazed their lips over my ear.

"Hello little flame."

Holy mother of God. It was them. I could hardly believe it. It wasn't possible. Aries' eyes were the first ones I saw.

"Aries'..."-

Orion put his finger to my lips.

"No names, little flame. One night, then you go your way, we go ours, understand?"

I nodded.

"I need your words, little flame," he rumbled.

"Ye..yes.."-

"Good girl."

They led me to a room, and Orion took charge. The way he looked at me when I called him daddy had me nearly coming without him even touching me. Of all of them, it's Orion who definitely has the 'daddy vibes'. I was almost in a daze the entire time, and when Orion finished fucking me, they cleaned me up and brought me wine and food.

Orion kissed my temple. "That's a good girl. We need to keep your strength up. We have a long night ahead of us."

Holy fuck.

Once I had eaten and used the restroom, Leo guided me to the bed, laying me on my back. Three sets of eyes looked at me as if I were a feast set out for them. Despite the way they were all looking at me, I kept reminding myself this was only one night. Then I'd leave for Amsterdam. I had no idea when I'd see them again, or if I ever would. I didn't know which was worse: seeing them and knowing what we did but never having that again, or cutting ties all together. Orion made the rules crystal clear at the beginning of the night. I pushed the thought aside, focusing on the present and the three? Or was it four? Mind blowing orgasms I'd already had.

"It's my turn to fuck this tight little pussy," Leo rumbled. His golden lion mask made his amber eyes even more intense as he licked me from my belly button to my nipples, sucking on them, making my pussy flutter. His cock hit my entrance, and he fucked me like a man possessed. His eyes never leaving mine as Orion and Aries watched.

"Look at them, watching me fuck you, little flame," he rumbled. "Does that excite you?"

"Yes," I moaned as he kissed my neck and nipped at my ear. Orion and Aries were on either side of me, both watching Leo fuck me.

"Such a good girl taking all of my cock," he praised. His thrusts got harder and faster, and I wrapped my legs around his hips. And he bottomed out as Orion and Aries sucked on my nipples, sending shockwaves through my body, and I shattered, trying my damndest not to scream out Leo's name. My pussy fluttered around his cock and I felt his release.

He kissed me, drawing his teeth against my neck.

"My turn, sweetheart," Aries rumbled. He reached for my wrist, lifted me over his shoulder, his fingers playing with my pussy as he stalked over to one of the chairs, bending me over and smacking my ass.

"You don't know how many times I've wanted to do this to you," he rumbled in my ear as I shivered. "Bend you over and fuck you raw," he rumbled as he thrust himself inside me, and I screamed as he grasped my hips and fucked me hard and deep, hitting the spot over and over until I saw stars and I exploded. But he wasn't done; he reached under, flicking my clit, and another orgasm ripped through me. My pussy clenched around his cock, and he growled as I felt him come inside me.

"Such a good girl," he murmured, kissing my spine. He lifted me and walked us into the bathroom. He cleaned me up and then put me in the middle of them. Orion to my right, Leo to my left, and Aries above me. My eyes fluttered, and Orion's lips grazed my ear.

"Sleep for a little bit; we'll wake you."

Orion

Andee was sound asleep between Leo and me, Aries at the head of the bed. There we were, surrounding this tiny little creature like sentinels. Her cheeks were rosy, her hair was wild, and she looked freshly fucked. The look in Leo's eyes had me cocking my brow at him.

"Don't," I whispered, so I wouldn't wake Andee.

"What?" He balked.

"Don't what me. I know that look; I've known you entirely too long."

Aries was silent; he brushed Andee's hair away from her cheek.

"This was a bad idea," Aries said, sounding completely and utterly defeated.

I shook my head. "No. It's what was needed. Now we can let her live her life, like she should."

"What if whoever was after Atlas goes after her?" Leo asked.

"We have people all over Europe ready to be her 'neighbors.' And we will have surveillance at every house she's renting."

"And if she headed off to Germany for a weekend, then what?" Leo challenged.

I rumbled at Leo. "Not you, too? Tonight only," I said firmly, not wanting them to argue anymore. I didn't want to admit to them or myself that I was having second, third, and fourth thoughts as well. We let her sleep for an hour, then Atlas woke her by flicking her clit with his tongue. Her delicious little whimpers in her half-sleep state went straight to my cock. Her eyes popped open, and she looked down at Aries, her lips tipped into a smile as she tangled her hands in his hair and fucked herself on his tongue. Her sounds had me pumping my cock.

"I want you to come on Aries' tongue, little girl, then you're going to take what I give you, understand?"

"Yes, Daddy," she moaned, and fuck if I didn't nearly lose it with the words coming out of her bratty little mouth. We had four more hours with her, and I was going to make them count.

She was out. We had mis-counted the number of glasses of wine she had, and we knew by the state of her, she'd be asleep for hours. Each of us only dared to kiss her once. Any more, and all of my resolve would have gone out the window. I lifted her off the bed as Aries opened the door. This was killing me. My heart literally squeezing in my chest as I set her in the car with Daphne. Daphne's gaze on me and the others told me she wasn't happy we were ending things like this with Andee, but she didn't say anything.

The first time Andee fell asleep, Aries stalked out of the room, and when he came back. Daphne was with him. Thank fuck he knocked on the door quietly first.

We walked into the hall, and Daphne had a devious smile on her face. "I knew it was you," she teased.

"Yeah, well," Leo said.

"About fucking time," she huffed.

My smile faded, and Aries explained what we had planned. Daphne's brows furrowed deeper and deeper as Aries spoke. By the time he was done, she looked like she was going to kill all of us.

"She loves you all, *you assholes*," Daphne bit out.

Leo and Aries looked like they were going to be sick; I felt like a total dickhead.

"And you fuckers love her. So what's the problem?" Daphne's foot was tapping furiously on the marble floor, like a bomb waiting to go off.

"Daphne, this was crossing a line as it is. She needs to live her life."

"And you think putting her on a fucking plane alone without saying anything to her is a good fucking idea? You three may be some of the smartest men in the world, but with this, you've got your heads up your asses!"

"That's why I came to get you," Aries said with a tone of complete embarrassment. "We want you to go with her. All expenses paid. You can work from the office in Amsterdam, yes?"

"Yes," she answered tersely.

Aries had very much not told us about his little plan, but I had to admit it made me feel a little better. No less guilty, though. Daphne agreed, but only after calling us things I've only heard dangerous men say, and her glare cut through me as we set Andee in the car.

"You three are going to regret this. She's never going to forgive you. Nor should she." Her eyes cut right through me as she shut the door.

The three of us were silent on the way home. None of us spoke even when we walked in the door of the condo. We walked up the stairs and went into our rooms, shutting the doors behind us. Daphne was right. She would never forgive us. And I didn't know how I'd live with that, but I knew I deserved it.

Andee

One month later

Daphne yelled down the stairs, reminding me that it was supposed to rain and not to forget my rain jacket. We'd been living in a little house near a winding river in Amsterdam for the past month. When I woke up on the plane, Daphne held me until I had no tears left. I knew it was one night, but the way they ended it broke my heart. I lay in bed for a week, watching every sappy romance movie on the planet. Daphne dragged me out of bed, making me face the fact that I had to move on with my life. And after calling her many nasty things, I knew she was right.

We spent our days at the museums and taking day trips to different towns along the rivers that flowed through Amsterdam. Daphne's law firm had offices all over the world, and she took advantage of them. Her dad wasn't too thrilled at first, but she told him it was allow her to work like that or she'd quit. He chose the former. I had enough money for both of us to never work again if we chose, but she told me she didn't want to be a 'trophy wife,' and when we stopped laughing, she got back to a case she was working on. She works in the corporate law division, the most boring division in my opinion, but she loves it, and that's all that matters. I had my best friend, and an entire world to explore with her. I was putting the men out of my head.

That is until I got sick one night after dinner. Daphne held my hair back as I puked more than once. I had no other symptoms, so we figured it was food poisoning. I wish it had been that easy.

"How much more time?" I asked for the third time in less than a minute; I was literally shaking.

"One second less than a second ago," she said with a tiny eye roll. She was just as anxious as I was.

The timer went off, and I really felt sick.

"I can't look," I said, pushing the test toward Daphne.

"Eww!" She screeched. "Please move your pee stick away from me."

"It's covered!"

"I stand firm in my disgust," she teased.

I moved the 'pee stick' away from her.

She cursed under her breath.

My shoulders fell.
I crumpled to the floor.
She held me as sobs wracked my body.
I didn't deserve her in my life.

"You don't have to decide right now," she whispered once I was out of tears and we had moved into my bedroom, a pint of ice cream between us, and some movie playing in the background.

"I need time to process," I told her.

"I get that. This is a strange predicament."

"That's the understatement of the century," I said around a spoonful of ice cream.

"I don't understand; you were on the pill."

I shrugged. "Clearly, I'm the exception to the ninety-nine percent effectiveness rule."

"Either that, or one of them has super swimmers," she snorted.

"Oh my God! You did not just say that!" I tossed a pillow at her, and she dodged it, tossing it back.

We laughed until my belly ached, then I let out a sigh.

"What am I going to do, Daphne?"

She reached for my hand. "Whatever you decide, I'm here for you."

"I love you, you know that?"

"Obviously," she said in her stickiest, sweetest voice. "I love you back."

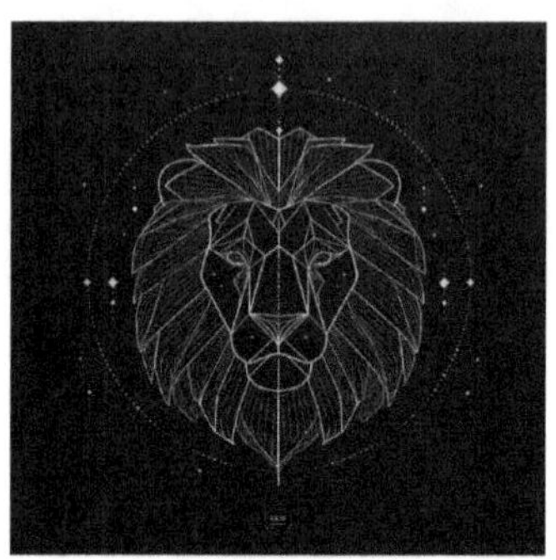

Leo

Eleven months later

How you talked me into this is beyond me," I told Aries. "If Orion finds out, he will murder both of us, you know that, right? He knows how to kill a man like thirty ways."

Aries laughed. "We do too, dummy."

"Yeah, but he's a lot faster."

Aries snorted.

"We aren't going to say anything; I just need to see her."

I wasn't going to argue; I needed it as much as he did.

Andee had been living with Daphne in a small little house in Amsterdam for the past eleven months. Two weeks in, she ripped out all our equipment. But not before playing with herself and coming in front of our camera. Once she finished, she walked toward the camera, flipped us off, and yanked it out of the wall. Daphne finally answered my call three days later, telling us we were assholes. They replaced the system, buying from our competition, which stung, but at least they had a security system.

We cracked Atlas' codebook and figured out he was talking to the one mafia organization that owned more property than we did. Enzo Romano. Head of the entire Cosa Nostra, and not just in the USA. He was a scary fucker, and we're pretty scary ourselves. Over the past six months, patterns had emerged. Orion caught the first acquisitions, small, high-level security firms purchased through layers of shell corporations that never changed the public face of the business. The CEOs stayed. The staff stayed. Only the infrastructure shifted quietly underneath. It was Romano's organization. So we countered. Spending the past six months crisscrossing the globe buying companies before he could get to them, using shell companies of our own. Sales stayed private, our contract sealing the company's fate. We bought several of them out, pulled some under the umbrella of our company, but some refused to play ball. Romano had gotten to them first.

The thing pissing us off the most was the fact that the fucker was always two steps ahead of us. We'd get a company to sell or buy out, thinking we were getting ahead, only for Romano to swipe up two more right from under us. Then, he went after one of the firms we had represented for years. It was a bold move, but one that we stopped easily. But that was the point. Romano wanted to prove he could if he chose to, and that put us on more alert than we'd ever been. We turned our entire company upside down, switching every program, software system, computer, safety protocol, everything. But Romano would still be ahead of us. We finally chalked it up to his mafia connections. We had our own connections, but not in the same way he did. His network in the seedy underbelly of the major cities far outweighed ours.

We avoided Amsterdam like the fucking plague. Until we couldn't. Van der Voss Securities ran software that allowed emergency response permissions across countries and had government contracts with every government in Europe. It would cost a lot, but we couldn't let Romano get his hands on it. So, Orion told us he was going to Amsterdam, and we didn't let the asshat leave us in the states.

"I know where you two are, you assholes," Orion's gravelly voice came through the phone.

"We weren't hiding it from you," Aries lobbed back.

"Then why didn't you tell me?" He rasped.

"Cause you would have tried to talk us out of it."

"Exactly," he rasped.

"It's not good for any of us, and you know it."

We looked at each other. He was right. I hated to admit it, but he was. "We'll be back for the meeting," I sighed.

"Good. See you then."

We were stuck on the main highway into the city, a six car pile-up on the bridge, when my phone rang.

"Where the fuck are you?" Orion growled.

"Still in traffic. Why do you sound so grumpy?"

"Romano got to them. They let me dance around for a half-hour before they admitted it. The fucker was bold this time. Had me meet with the CEO, then *after* fucking with me, Romano's nephew walked in as if he'd been working there for years."

"I mean, this isn't the first time it's happened," I said.

We'd gotten used to not dwelling on the losses and just moving on; it took too much energy and resources.

"This one is different."

"Why?" Aries asked.

"Van der Voss is the system in her house."

"Fuck! I hissed, "We aren't going anywhere in this traffic; we're halfway on the bridge."

"I'll go," Orion said. I'll stop by the office and get new equipment."

"She's going to be pissed."

"I don't give a fuck."

"Are you going to do this and be able to walk away again?"

My question hung in the air.

"I don't have a choice."

Andee

A week after I found out, I sat at the clinic, Daphne sitting by my side, holding my hand. I didn't think I could do it. How could I raise a child that looked like one of them? Seeing one of their faces every day, I thought it would be too hard. But when the nurse called me, I rushed out the door of the clinic. We sat in a small park until it was completely dark, the sky full of stars. And a shooting star streaked across the sky. Only one. Right across Cassiopeia. Daphne called me crazy. I took it as a sign. When Cassie was born, there was no question who her father was. The moment her eyes opened, I saw Orion, and I cried. I loved all of them, wanted to be with all of them, but he was, well..

"I still can't believe your mommy named you Cassiopeia," Daphne cooed over my daughter as she changed her diaper.

"You're a terrible influence on her," I called across our tiny house as I took some pacifiers out of the dishwasher.

"At least when she's older, I can tell her it was all you picking her name."

"What? Cassie is sweet."

"When she's in school, they won't call her Cassie on the first day, *Andromeda*."

"I survived, so will she. Besides, it's on brand."

"You are so weird."

I threw a burp cloth over my shoulder, ready to feed Cassie, and there was a knock at the door.

"Are you expecting anyone?" I called to Daphne.

"Oh! Mrs. Anderson said she wanted to drop off a gift for the baby."

"She's too sweet," I said.

I opened the door. It wasn't Mrs. Anderson, far from it. I was frozen. The pacifier slipped out of my hand, and he caught it. His eyes burned into mine. Neither of us saying anything, and my knees almost buckled.

"Is it Mrs. Anderson?" Daphne called out, rounding the corner with Cassie.

I couldn't speak because of the lump in my throat.

"No. No it is not," Orion rumbled.

Daphne's eyes widened. "Oh, shit," she murmured.

Oh, shit was right.

Orion walked past me, straight to Daphne. One look at the baby and I knew he knew she was his. Daphne looked at me silently, as if asking me what she should do.

"Give her to me," Orion rasped.

Daphne turned away from Orion. "Not before you wash your hands," she bit out.

He sighed and stalked into the kitchen.

"What are you doing?" I whisper hissed.

She shrugged her shoulders. "I don't know? I panicked! It's not like he didn't see her or anything. What was I supposed to do?"

Orion strode back into the hall, taking Cassie from Daphne. Her tiny hand literally wrapped around his finger. Fuck. Why does the universe hate me?

I thought he was hot as fuck before, but holding the baby, forget ruined panties. I swear my ovaries fluttered. His eyes never left Cassie, but then he looked at me. Not with anger, almost apologetically, but there was hurt behind his eyes too. I felt like a complete asshole.

"Her name is Cassie."

Daphne scoffed. "She named her Cassiopeia."

Orion looked at me, then at Cassie. "It's perfect."

Daphne threw her hands up in the air. "You people and your names! I mean, what the fuck?"

"You clearly never spent any time in a British boarding school," Orion said as he shrugged off his coat, pulled a burp cloth off the counter and sat in one of the chairs like he fucking owned the place.

Flutter I was so fucked.

He took his phone out of his pocket and pressed a button. "You still stuck in traffic?" He asked the person on the other line calmly, keeping his voice even.

"We just broke through, why?"

Leo.

"I need you to come to the house. There's been a complication."

"With the new system?"

Aries.

Of course they were together; why couldn't it just be one of them? Because that's how my fucking life works, that's why.

Orion snapped a photo, and the sound of about twenty cars honking and Leo cursing filled the air.

"Don't kill yourselves, but get here."

"That wasn't a U-turn lane!" Leo screamed at Aries.

"I don't give a fuck!"

Orion's lips tilted in that way that always made my knees weak. "See you soon." He hung up the phone.

Then I realized. He said, 'the house.'

"You asshole," I hissed at him. He peered up at me. "You've been keeping tabs on me, haven't you?" My eyes narrowed at him, and I literally growled.

"Well, sweetheart, after your little *show*."

My cheeks heated. My drunk revenge performance. I had no idea I was pregnant, of course. Daphne laughed her ass off after she woke me up and told her what I did. She teased me for being a lightweight, 'getting drunk' on two glasses of wine.

"We had to make sure you were safe."

"No. You didn't," I bit out at him.

He didn't take his eyes off me.

"You sent me away. You lost the right to check on me."

"You agreed to the rules, same as us."

Low blow, asshole.

"And you put me in a car without as much as a goodbye."

I can hit back just as low.

Orion and Daphne shared a look. But then Orion turned back to Cassie, who started crying.

"Give her here," I said.

He just looked at me.

"She needs to eat," I said with a 'duh' look on my face.

His eyes never left me as he handed me the baby. I sat in the glider rocker and fed her. Cassie grasped my hand, and I held it, the two of us in our own little bubble. As soon as Cassie was asleep, Orion nearly yanked her out of my arms. Not really, but the determination in his eyes told me not to argue. I watched him with her, and I didn't even realize Leo and Aries had walked in. They both looked at me, and I broke. One of them was bad enough. All three together? It was too much. Daphne nodded, and I climbed the stairs and retreated into my room. I heard her tell Aries to get the fuck away from the stairs or she'd string him up by his nuts; a laugh spilled out, but only for a second or two. I crashed onto my bed and curled into a ball.

I cried over them more nights than I could count. I was just getting over them when I found out I was going to have Cassie. All nine months I would push the thought of them aside whenever she kicked me or moved, determined to do it on my own. I couldn't rely on them. Daphne was the only constant in my life.

It was us against the world, and I needed to keep it that way.

Aries

When Orion sent the picture of the tiny little creature who had his eyes, I nearly crashed the car. I'd turned around like I was Mario fucking Andretti.

"She's Orion's," Leo said with a touch of jealousy in his tone. I was feeling the same way.

"Doesn't matter though," I said as another driver honked at me as I raced around them.

"I'd like not to die before we get there, if that's alright with you?" Leo snarked.

"We're fine!" I rasped out as a truck driver flipped me off.

Leo stared at me. "Your nuts, you know that, right?"

I just smiled and kept moving between cars, getting at least ten more honks and three more birds flipped at me.

Leo let out a breath. "No, I guess it doesn't matter. You know what Orion is going to do. She's not going to be happy."

"We'd do the same, and like I said, doesn't matter. She belongs to us. She always has."

Neither of us said what we were really thinking about Andee's safety. Almost a year had passed, and nothing had come. No move against us, nothing direct against Andee, and that silence was worse than anything else. We knew it was the Romanos behind Atlas' murder, but aside from one attempted breech of one of our companies, they'd done nothing, and that kind of restraint didn't make us less wary, it made us more determined to figure out what Atlas been involved in, and why they'd suddenly changed the way they played.

Leo blew out a breath. "Why didn't she tell us?"

"We left her. Sent her away without as much as a good-bye," I said. The guilt had been picking at me more and more the longer we were away from her. "Can you blame her?"

Leo pinched the bridge of his nose, leaning his head back. "No, I suppose not." He was quiet for a minute. "How many times did you nearly say *fuck it* and go after her?" Leo asked quietly.

My eyes flicked to his for a second. "More times than I can count," I admitted.

"Same."

The little white house with blue shutters came into view. I was more nervous than I had ever been in my entire life. Leo and I climbed the steps; I automatically reached for the handle and opened the door. There she was; she took my breath from my lungs. Tears filled her eyes when she saw us, and it broke my heart. She looked at Daphne, and then she climbed the narrow staircase and disappeared from sight.

I strode to the steps; Daphne blocked my way. "Daphne," I warned with a rumble.

"Aries, I swear to fuck, if you so much as even take one more step toward those stairs, I will string you up by your nuts." Daphne's face was full of anger and I sighed, turning to see Leo standing near Orion who was holding the baby, like he'd done it a million times.

I sighed and walked into the small living room.

Leo touched the baby's hand, and Daphne cursed. "Wash your fucking hands!"

Both of us winced, but crossed the small space, hung up our coats, and walked into the galley kitchen. We took turns washing our hands, then went back into the living room. Orion had the baby on his shoulder. There was no doubt she was his.

"What's her name?" I asked, swallowing the lump in my throat.

"Cassiopeia," Daphne hissed. "But we call her Cassie," she added.

The little thing couldn't have been more than a month old, or so. I looked at Daphne.

"You three fuckers did this to yourselves," she huffed. "Do you know how many nights she cried herself to sleep because of you? More than I can fucking count. And before you say it, no, she should *not* have told you. Leave her the fuck alone," she spat, her eyes flicking toward the stairs.

"Daphne," Orion said with a warning, but even tone.

"Orion," Daphne answered with no fear in her voice.

The two stared at one another.

"She loved you, all of you, and you broke her. She loves that little girl more than life itself, but the sadness in her eyes every time she looks at Cassie, seeing your eyes looking back at her, it's killing her."

I felt like the biggest asshole in the world. And I deserved it.

Daphne literally growled at Orion when he tried to take Cassie upstairs. She put her hands out, and the look on her face was more than murderous intent, so he passed the baby to her. Orion was sleeping in an overstuffed chair that was way too small for his six-foot-six frame. Leo was on the lumpy ass couch and I was on the floor. Feeling my age when my back cracked as I got up from the floor to use the bathroom. I crept up the stairs and quietly opened Andee's door. She was asleep, Cassie sleeping curled against her. I slid into the bed next to them. Andee's scent of roses and rain enveloped me. She was radiant. Even more beautiful and fierce than the last time we saw her.

Cassie started fussing, and Andee opened her eyes, but they weren't focused on the baby. They were focused on me.

"You shouldn't be here, Aries," she whispered. She turned her attention to Cassie, with calming sounds, trying to get her back to sleep. But she started crying. Andee picked her up, leaned against the headboard, and nursed her. "Shhh," she cooed.

It was the most beautiful sight I'd ever seen in my life. I sat up and leaned against the headboard, just entranced by the sight.

"Why are you here, Aries?" She asked quietly, her eyes never leaving the baby.

I reached my hand out, caressing her cheek. She leaned into my touch, and my entire body relaxed for the first time in almost a year. "We were stupid, stupid men," I admitted with a quiet sigh. "We never should have left you that way."

Her eyes narrowed. Fuck.

"Shit," I murmured. "What I meant to say..."-

She shook her head, "No. You meant it, clearly. Maybe you're sorry you left me that way, but that was always the way it was going to be. Don't insult me by pretending otherwise."

"I didn't want to leave you, kitten," I murmured. She moved away slightly, and my hand dropped.

Tears filled her eyes. "Fuck," she murmured, swiping them away. "I can't do this right now, Aries. You need to leave."

She moved the baby to the other side, and I slowly rose from the bed and slipped out of the room. I plopped on the third to last step. I wanted to go back and be with her, beg her to forgive us until she did. None of us had been with any other woman since her. We didn't even bother to try. There was no one else for us. Even Orion admitted it a few months back.

"What's wrong with you?" Leo asked, handing me a mug of coffee.

"Got anything stronger?" I half joked as I stood.

Leo laughed, and we walked into the living room. Orion was massaging his neck, letting out a long groan as it cracked.

"Hey old man," Leo chuckled.

"Fuck off," Orion rumbled as he cracked his back. He stalked into the kitchen, poured himself a cup of coffee, and his eyes flicked upstairs when he heard the baby. Leo and I joined him in the kitchen, and we all sat around the little wooden table near the window.

Orion let out a long sigh. The man was a master at brooding. He could have done it professionally, I swear.

"How are you feeling?" Leo asked, his tone cautious.

"How do you think I feel? Like an asshole, pissed at myself, trying not to blame her for keeping this from us."

Us. Relief filled me when he didn't just say 'me.' I could tell Leo was feeling the same way.

"We deserve her ire, and more," I admitted.

Orion's face was unreadable as he took another sip of his coffee. Daphne came down the stairs, poured a cup of coffee for herself, her eyes narrowed as she took a sip.

"Dammit, you're still here. I was hoping yesterday was just a really fucked up dream." Her smile was almost deadly as she sipped her coffee.

"Hilarious, Daphne," Leo balked.

"You three have just upended our existence. We were doing just fine without you. And we'll do fine once you're gone, so thanks for stopping by. Don't let the door hit you on the ass when you leave; the place is a rental."

"Not going to happen, Daphne," Orion rumbled.

"Exactly what do you think is going to happen here, Orion? Do you think she wants anything to do with you three?"

"She doesn't have a choice." Orion's eyes narrowed when the words came out of his mouth.

Daphne balked. "HA! The fuck she doesn't."

"There's only one choice here, Daphne, especially because she's raising my child."

Fuck. That hurt. But when he looked at me and Leo, I knew he was just making a point.

"She doesn't want you here. Can't you just respect her wishes, for Christ's sake?"

When he didn't answer, a loud grumble escaped her lips, followed by muttered curses.

She turned to leave, then turned back. Her eyes narrowed. "You hurt her, hurt them, and I will murder you all myself." She turned and stomped out of the kitchen.

"Andee is not going to like this at all," Leo said.

Orion's face was extremely nonchalant. "She doesn't have a choice."

"The fuck I don't, Orion," Andee hissed as she rounded the corner, Cassie in her arms.

Fuck me, she had fire in her eyes, and she was fierce as fuck. Like a mama bear protecting her cub. It made my cock twitch, and I wasn't mad about it.

Orion

Of all the things I thought I would encounter seeing Andee for the first time in almost a year, a baby was very much *not* on my bingo card. When the pacifier dropped out of her hand, I silently hoped the baby wasn't Daphne's. Does that make me a possessive asshole? Yes. Do I give a fuck? Not in the slightest. The moment I looked into Cassie's eyes, I knew she was mine. Andee looked like she was going to either kiss me or kill me; I wasn't sure, but I wasn't really paying attention. All I saw was the tiny little creature I was holding in my arms. My heart squeezed when I thought about Andee looking at our daughter every day and seeing my eyes.

Daphne's words from that night still haunted me. *"You three are going to regret this. She's never going to forgive you. Nor should she."*

After the night at the club, I threw myself into work, sometimes sleeping in my office, anything to distract me from thinking about her. But sleep was almost worse. Every time I closed my eyes, I saw her face. I didn't tell Aries and Leo I had nearly gone after her more than a dozen times over the past few months. We didn't deserve her, and when she looked at me, telling me I had no right to check on her, that we had left her, being the asshole I am, I mentioned the rules she agreed to the night at the club.

We finally cracked Atlas' codebook and found out he had been talking to Enzo Romano, the head of the Cosa Nostra. And over the past year, besides one attempt at breeching our system, they didn't come for us, or Andee. It sat wrong with all of us; them staying so quiet. It didn't make us feel safer; it made us want to know why. Romano had more resources, more contacts, more spies, more networks than we did, ten to one.

Early on, I certain we had a mole in our midst, but after three months of changing everything, and vetting every single employee to make sure they weren't the source, we realized Romano had over seventy years of networks in place because of how long his family has been the head of the Cosa Nostra, while we had just over twenty. Plus, Romano had access to the underbelly of the cities he controlled. His currency was secrets, and he had a lot in the bank.

There was still one code none of us could crack. And we couldn't spend the time on it we wanted because we were globe hopping for the past six months.

"This is not his endgame," I told Leo and Aries one night, about five months ago. "He's got something bigger planned. I just don't know what it is."

"He's saving us for last," Leo balked.

"The protocols we put into place will make everything we have obsolete if they try anything."

"I still worry about them going after her," Leo murmured.

I looked at him. I was too.

"Locking that shit up inside you is worse than smoking three packs of cigarettes a day, you know," Aries taunted with a wily smile.

I rolled my eyes at him and got back to work. I knew the last code was the key to opening everything; we just had to get to it.

❖ ❖ ❖

"Andee is not going to like this at all," Leo said.

I was very matter-of-fact in my tone. "She doesn't have a choice."

"The fuck I don't, Orion," Andee hissed as she rounded the corner, the baby in her arms.

The fire in her eyes was drawing me like a moth to a flame. All the things stopping me before were wiped away the moment I laid eyes on the baby. I didn't just want Andee; I needed her. She was like the air I needed to breathe, and I knew the moment our eyes met the day before, the tightness in my chest I'd been feeling since we put her in that car was my body not having what it needed.

Her.

I stood and closed the distance between Andee and me. I touched Cassie's little cheek and then my eyes flicked to Andee. She hadn't taken her eyes off me. I put the tips of my fingers under her chin, trying to concentrate on the task at hand and not my aching cock.

"You will come with us, little flame. It's not up for discussion."

She tried to yank her chin from my grasp, but I was immovable. Her eyes narrowed.

"You don't own me, Orion," she hissed.

My lips brushed against her ear. "That's where you're wrong, little flame. We always did."

Her eyes widened, and she literally growled at me.

I stood at my full height. I towered over Andee; we all did. Her head tilted, and she glared right through me.

"Now, either you start packing, or I will have someone come in and do it for you. It's your choice."

Her lips thinned and her jaw clenched. "Fine," she hissed. The word dripping with venom.

She turned to walk upstairs.

"Good girl."

She stopped dead in her tracks. Her head turned slowly. "Don't." She said calmly. Her tone hit me more than if she had growled or screamed at me; then she continued walking up the stairs.

Leo let out a long whistle; Aries shook his head.

"This is bad," Aries said.

"We have to earn her trust back," Leo murmured.

I hoped with my entire being that would be the case. At least trust us enough not to want to want to rip our heads off.

If looks could kill, I'd be dead. Daphne glowered at me for most of the flight from Amsterdam to Spain.

We rarely stayed at our villa near the coast, but it was the safest location for all of us, while still having the tech capabilities we needed. Perched on a cliff above the turquoise Mediterranean waters, the villa looked impossibly remote, as if it had grown out of the rocks themselves, and we used that to our advantage. From the road below, it was nearly invisible, by design. Walls of glass reflected the clear blue sky; jagged stone terraces blended seamlessly with the natural cliffs, and carefully landscaped greenery hid every path and entrance. We insured security was woven into the architecture. Hidden cameras framed every angle, motion sensors traced the entire perimeter, and a discreet private jetway allowed our arrivals and departures far from prying eyes.

The jet landed, and Edward had two cars ready for us. I had called him right after Andee had walked up the stairs, insuring her room was between mine and Leo's, then I called Harrison and had a door between the rooms installed. Aries rumbled when I told him he'd have to move to the room directly behind Andee's, but when he realized there would be a door between those rooms as well, he stopped his grumbling. It was so that we could help Andee with Cassie. Or at least that's what I was telling myself. Andee's eyebrows narrowed when I told her about the door, but I expected that. That first time I saw her nursing Cassie, and it was the most incredible thing I had ever seen in my life. It made me realize just how much we had fucked up. I was in love with her, and we crushed her. It was killing me.

Daphne insisted on helping Andee settle in, so the three of us went out to the terrace overlooking our private beach, all of us quietly drowning our shame in our drinks.

"When was the last time we were here?" Aries asked, almost wistfully, trying to strike up as normal a conversation as possible.

I drew from my drink. "Maybe five years?" I shrugged.

Aries grinned. "Oh, right, the Tabitha debacle."

Leo's laugh echoed in my ears.

I narrowed my brows. "We don't talk about that, remember?" I said in a warning tone.

Tabitha Moroni was a woman who actually piqued my interest enough to actually try having a relationship. We dated for six months, and I brought her here for a long weekend. She attended the governor's gala with me, and I caught her fucking one of our rivals in the coat closet. I never shared company information, but I threatened to sue her if she revealed anything, anyway. After hacking into her phone, she quickly agreed.

"Anyway, besides that, the last one to be here was Atlas. He brought Maeve here trying to get in with a specialist."

"Oh, that's right. I forgot," Leo said with a smile. "We stayed at Atlas' condo with Andee."

Aries chuckled. "Talk about foreshadowing."

"You are a very disturbed individual, you know that, right?" Leo shook his head at Aries, who just laughed.

We sat enjoying the quiet until Daphne came out to ask about nappies for the baby, or 'diapers' as she called them. I rang Sophia, the house manager. Daphne balked at my 'pretentious staffing choices' and then Sophia walked onto the terrace.

Aries' eyes followed Daphne and Sophia.

"What?" I asked.

"I didn't say anything."

"Tell that to your face," I chuckled.

He let out a long breath. "We never really talked about how this would all work," he murmured, as if afraid to bring it up. There were a lot of questions hanging over us, and hadn't really worked most of them out.

"We let her take the lead," I said.

Leo scoffed. "That's only *if* she ever stops looking like she wants to murder us and bury us in the backyard. I know Daphne would help dig the hole. She's scary as fuck."

Aries cleared his throat. "And the other thing?"

"My blood flowing through Cassie's veins doesn't change anything; Andee is ours, she always was. The moment her lips captured all of us, there was no other choice."

"About fucking time," Aries scoffed.

"Don't. You're just as guilty."

"Okay, Mr. Broody. Sure. You've always been the one who pulled back the hardest."

He wasn't wrong. But I didn't back down.

"What stopped you, Aries?" I taunted.

His eyes widened. "What stopped me?" He hissed. "You! You prick!"

"You're an adult; you didn't need my permission." I lobbed back.

Aries rose from his chair, towering over me. "You have always taken the lead. When Leo and I went to check on her in Amsterdam before the meeting, what did you say?" His eyes narrowed.

I let out a breath, unable to answer him.

He scoffed as he sat back down. "That's what I thought."

For the next hour, none of us spoke; we just pretended everything was the way it should be. We had gotten to be experts at it.

Andee

"Neanderthals," I hissed under my breath.

"At least you're not talking to yourself," Daphne chuckled as she walked into the bedroom and tossed me a diaper.

"The 'house manager'," she rolled her eyes, "Sophia, told me to have you write down anything you need for the baby. Though Orion didn't waste any time, did he?" She said with a low whistle.

The room was perfect. Painted navy blue to match the sky, and all the constellations were painted on the ceiling. Orion must have had painters here working overnight to get it done. The room had a bassinet with navy and pink tulle, a glider rocking chair, an overstuffed chair, and everything else one could dream up for a nursery. The other half of the giant room was a king sized bed, and everything I could ever need or want. And there was also another room for Cassie, one door away. As much as it tugged at my heartstrings, it also pissed me off to no end.

"Are you okay? Smoke's practically coming out of your ears," she chuckled.

"I just.. I mean, they just... Grr!" I hissed out.

"You actually thought they'd let you be?"

Daphne plopped into the overstuffed chair, pulling the white teddy bear out from behind her back and holding it against her chest. "And can you blame them?" She almost said wistfully.

I cocked a brow at her as I snapped Cassie's little pink onesie.

"You're not going soft on me, are you?"

She cracked a smile. "No, never."

"That's what I thought; you had me worried for a second."

"All kidding aside, Andee, they are good men, all of them. Even if they made terrible choices because of, let's be honest, your dad."

"There you go, making sense. I'd thank you not to, if you don't mind."

She rose from the chair, crossed the room, picked Cassie up and laid her against her chest. She put her hand on my arm. "Did they fuck up? Yes. More than what should be forgivable. But you've had it bad for these men since you were what? Sixteen?"

I laughed. "fourteen."

She drew in an overdramatic breath. "You little harlot," she laughed.

"It was when Orion gave me my 'birthday kiss' on the cheek, and I felt a flutter in my stomach. It freaked me the fuck out. That's why I didn't say anything. I knew it was wrong, and I thought something was wrong with me."

She squeezed my hand. "Is it unconventional? Yes. Will people think it's inappropriate, even though you're all fucking adults? One million percent."

"You're not really helping your argument, Daph," I teased.

She rolled her eyes at me. "The point I'm trying to make is you're the only ones that matter and fuck the rest of the world."

"How do I choose just one of them, especially with.."-

"You don't, kitten."

Aries stalked across the room, placed his hands on ei-ther side of my face and kissed me like he needed me like he needed air to breathe, and my knees nearly buckled. He wrapped his arms around me, pulling me closer, but never stopped kissing me, not until I broke the kiss because I had run out of air.

"Aries," I murmured against his chest.

Daphne slipped out of the room with Cassie, winking at me as she closed the door.

"I love you, Andee. I have since forever, and I thought I would burn in hell because of it. I denied it, lived with the emptiness, because I didn't realize you were not only a piece, but my entire soul."

Holy mother of God.

My lips crashed against Aries, his hands grabbed my ass, and he lifted me up, my legs going around his hips. He turned and threw the door open, laying me on his bed.

"Look at you," he rumbled, pulling my shorts and panties down. He lifted my top over my head and unhooked my very sensible nursing bra, which made my cheeks warm. He glowered at me. "You can nourish Cassie, and that is a fucking miracle, and might I add," he wiggled his eyebrows. "The most sexy thing I've ever seen." Before I could say anything, he kissed me again; my breasts came free. He pinched my very sensitive nipples, my pussy fluttered, and my back arched.

"Oh, I'm going to enjoy this," he said with a raw, unbridled look in his eyes. He got undressed, and his monster cock stood at attention as he dove between my thighs and fucked me with his tongue. My hands tangled in his hair as I moaned his name.

"Fuck, I love hearing my name on your lips, kitten," he murmured, and went back to fucking me with his tongue. My legs shook, and he chuckled, the vibration making me writhe against his mouth as he sucked on my clit so hard I saw shattered. He didn't stop; he pinched my nipples and sucked even harder, and my entire body shook. He kept at it until I finally stopped shaking.

"Holy fuck," I said, as I tried to catch my breath.

"Oh, kitten, I am not even close to being done with you. Now ride my cock like a good girl."

I apparently didn't move fast enough for his liking, and he lifted me to straddle him. My pussy slid down his cock and we both let out a satisfied sigh as I circled my hips, his stormy grey eyes watching me, as he played with my nipples. He let out a deep growl when my pussy clenched around his cock.

"Such a tight little pussy, milk my cock, baby girl," he murmured, and I ground against him clenching his cock as his hips moved up and down, his cock hitting the spot over and over until I saw white behind my eyes and I screamed out my release.

"Oh fuck! Aries, please don't stop, I'm coming..fucckk!"

His cock twitched, and he roared out my name as I felt him come inside me. I collapsed on his chest, and our ragged breaths filled the air as he kissed me, then rolled me onto our sides, still connected.

He brushed my wild hair out of my face and looked at me with such love, I barely kept it together.

"Can you ever forgive me, kitten?"

"Yes. I love you, Aries."

It's like I absolved him of his all his sins or something, because there was a shift in his eyes; he let out a sigh and pulled me against his chest.

"I'm not going to disappear, Aries," I teased, trying to get out of his arms. "I have to check on Daphne; she's had Cassie for... Oh my god! Three hours!"

He pulled me against him, and his lips brushed against my ear. "As much as I already love that little creature in the other room, and will protect her and you until I draw my last breath, we are getting her a nanny, sooner rather than later. Because I plan on having you in my bed as often as possible."

My body melted against his, and I turned to face him. "And I love you for that, but I think it's best if I stay in the other room, at least until I've settled things with Leo and Orion." I hated that my voice wavered when I said Orion's name. I lowered my eyes.

"Hey," Aries murmured, lifting my chin so I was looking into his stormy grey eyes. "You belong to us, kitten. All of us. And that means Cassie, too. I don't care that her DNA isn't the same as mine. She is mine, just as much as Orion and Leo. Besides, he chuckled. "The next one *will* share my DNA."

I cocked a brow at him. "And what makes you think that's ever happening, Aries Thorne?"

He nibbled my ear. "Because I said so," he rumbled, and fuck if my ovaries didn't do a little flip.

Down girls.

"Andee isn't even two months old, Aries. Think we can put a pin in that for a little while, at least?"

He literally considered my question, and I playfully batted his chest. "I'll think about it," he said with a chuckle. I tossed a pillow at him as I rolled out of the bed, got dressed, and opened the door to my room, laughing as I closed the door.

It was dark in my room, all except for the little moon shaped night light near Cassie's bassinet. And there he was. Sitting in the dark like he owned it, our daughter in his arms.

Flutter

I nearly made the mistake of asking him why he thought it was okay to be in the room, but I closed my mouth, thinking better of it. The reason was sitting in his arms. "We need to talk, little flame." His velvet, yet raspy voice did something to my insides that I wanted to hate. But I couldn't.

I crossed the room, flipping on the bedside lamp, letting soft light spill across the room. Orion Kane is a very tall, very muscular man. His jaw is like chiseled granite, with just a hint of stubble. But his eyes, they are such a deep blue any woman could drown in them, and I had. He was sin in a tailored suit and fuck if I didn't want to forget everything and let him do whatever he wanted to me. But I sat on my bed instead, hoping the distance would cool the fucking heat between my thighs.

"So, talk," I said, not daring to look at him, though I felt his eyes on me as he rose from the chair and laid Cassie in her bassinet. He closed the distance and reached for my hand. I pulled it away and his low rumble went straight to my pussy.

"I can't leave her.."-

He reached into his jacket pocket and handed me a baby monitor, a color fucking 4K baby monitor. I watched as my sweet girl's little mouth made little twitching movements. He reached for my hand again, and I rose from the bed, and his hand landed on the small of my back, and I shivered. His amused, dark chuckle went straight through me. This man was going to be the literal death of me. He reached for the knob on his door and let me walk in first. The room screamed Orion. It was classic yet modern; dark chocolate brown wood beams criss-crossed the ceiling, and everything was the same dark wood or deep green.

He sat in a chair near the window, the afternoon sun retreating. The entire sky bursting with every shade of pink and orange, like waves in the sky.

"It's beautiful here," I said, watching a sailboat lazily float by.

"It is. But I didn't bring you here to talk about the weather."

"Then what, Orion?"

All three of them had broken me. Aries had put some pieces back together, and I knew Leo would make things right between us. While Leo and Aries were immensely powerful, strong-willed men, Orion was the one who always got the last word in business, and most decisions that had to do with the three of them, and that excited and scared me at the same time. It always had.

But it was Orion who always could make me shatter with just one look.

"The little being in the next room."

"What about her?"

"We need to consider her safety and yours for the future."

I scoffed. "We're here, aren't we? Uprooted our lives because of your insistence," I bit out at him.

He nodded. "Yes, but that doesn't solve things in the long term."

"I don't know what you want from me, Orion."

I felt tears in my eyes, and I hated it. I had promised myself I'd never cry over him again. But there I was, tears burning my eyes because I refused to let them fall. His face was unreadable, but he put his hand out. And I fought every instinct to go to him.

I shook my head. "Do you know how hard it was, Orion, loving someone with your entire being, your entire soul, but each time you looked at them your heart shattered because their existence alone was both your salvation and your torment?" My eyes stung with unshed tears. I put my head in my hands and just let them just fucking fall.

I felt hands on my sides, and he boosted me up by my ass. My legs found their way around his waist like I'd done it a million times.

His lips brushed against my ear. "Yes, I do, and It's the worst pain imaginable."

My lips crashed into his, my hands tangling in his hair. His growl against my mouth made my pussy flutter. My back crashed against the wall, knocking the wind out of me as he held me up with one hand, as I heard his belt come undone. He pushed my shorts and panties aside and thrust his cock inside me.

Orion

Andee looked so little, like she didn't have any fight left in her. My restraint had been thinning from the moment I heard her and Aries in the next room. I went into Cassie's room to set up the baby monitor, Andee wasn't there. She was with Aries. Her breathy moans made me want it to be me and not him. When she returned, I tried to hold my shit together. But in my life, the one constant is my inability to keep myself together when it comes to Andee.

She stood near the floor-length window, and I had no idea why I said we had to talk. I just wanted an excuse to be in the same room as her. My questions were half-assed excuses for questions. When she asked what I wanted from her, I didn't have an answer, so I stayed silent. Then she shook her head.

"Do you know how hard it was, Orion, loving someone with your entire being, your entire soul, but each time you looked at them your heart shattered because their existence alone was both your salvation and your torment?"

Tears fell from her eyes, and her body shook. My resolve snapped, and the only thing that would allow me to be whole again was her. I closed the distance between us, lifting her under her perfect ass, and her legs wrapped around me, her heated little cunt rubbing against my cock.

My lips brushed against hers. "Yes, I do, and It's the worst pain imaginable."

Her lips crashed into mine, her hands in my hair, her hips moving against me. The growl I let out made her shutter as I pushed her against the wall. Holding her up with one arm, I unbelted myself, pushed her shorts and panties aside, and thrust inside her. She screamed my name, and I fucked her hard, my lips nipping her neck as I sunk into her sweet little pussy over and over. She was a drug that I needed in my veins; nothing else would sate me except her.

I railed into her over and over, "You were always mine," I growled in her ear as her lips grazed against my neck, and moans got louder as I continued to thrust inside her over and over and her pussy clenched my cock so hard her name ripped from my chest as I filled her with my cum, her body shattering around me, milking my cock, her body pulsing, her pussy fluttering as she came.

"Oh my God, Orion."

We were breathing hard, our breaths mingled as I kissed her deeply, grasping her ass so hard she'd have bruises, but I didn't care. Her moans softened, and I couldn't stop myself from kissing her. I walked us to the bed, and I laid her down, rolling us onto our sides. I pulled her shorts and panties off, lifting her shirt, and letting her beautiful breasts come free. I put her leg over my hip, thrusting inside her again.

"Orion, yesss," she hissed as she tipped her head back and I sucked her nipple so hard her entire body shook as our hips moved and I rubbed her clit with my finger. I fucked her slow and deep, and I watched her body reacting to me, and a possessive growl filled my chest.

"Fuckkk! Yes! I'm.."-

Her pussy clenched my cock like a vice as my cum filled her little pussy.

She rolled onto her back, and her arm fell over her eyes. "Holy fuck," she rasped.

After a couple of minutes, I lifted her, and she playfully batted my chest. "Orion, I am fully capable of walking to the bathroom."

"I didn't say you weren't," I rasped.

She rolled her eyes at me as I put her in the shower. The warm water trickled down her curves, and she raised onto her tiptoes and kissed me. Once we finished, I wrapped her in a towel, and she raised a brow at me when she tried to put her panties on. They were basically shredded. I pulled her into my arms. "My plan is to have you without clothes as much as I can, so there will be no need for them, anyway." A shiver went up her spine, and she sucked in a breath.

Once she was mostly dressed, I reached for her hand before she walked back into the other room.

"I should get back; Cassie will be up soon to eat."

I kissed her and looked into her beautiful blue eyes. "I love you," I told her. "I've fought it for too long, and I refuse to do so anymore."

A slight blush crept up her neck, and I loved it. "I love you too," she murmured.

I wanted to tell her to just bring the baby in here with me, but I knew she wanted to make things right with all of us first, so as much as I wanted to keep her with me, I let her go.

"Good night," she said with a soft murmur.

"Good night."

The following morning, I slipped into the Andee's room to check on the baby.

She was babbling to herself, just as happy as could be. I never intended on getting married, let alone having any children, so the little being in front of me was my chance to be a better man. Leave the world a better place for her and her mother. I lifted Cassie out of her bassinet and quietly changed her. Andee was sound asleep, and I didn't want to worry her, so I sat in the rocking chair, and Cassie just babbled away, and I was entranced. The world melted away, and it was just her and me.

Andee stirred, and as if Cassie knew her mother was up, she started fussing. Andee popped out of bed and had a surprised look, but then smiled and I switched places with her, handing the baby to her, and she cooed over her and while she fed Cassie. It was such a beautiful moment. I couldn't take my eyes off them.

"You're staring," she said, her attention never leaving Cassie.

"I can't help it."

Her eyes met mine, and she smiled.

"You look tired," I said, half teasing.

She cocked a brow at me. "I wonder why."

"We need to talk about getting a nanny."

"I'm not sure, Orion. I don't want to be one of those mothers who let the nannies raise the kids, only spending time with them between their trips around the world."

"How about I call an agency that are clients of ours. They've all been vetted by us already, so there won't be as much research or background checks needed."

She considered my idea. "Would the nanny live with us?"

"If you'd like. All three of us had live-in nannies," I told her.

She smirked. "That's the shock of the century."

I walked over to her, kissed her on the top of the head. "Let me get a list together at least."

She nodded and readjusted as I got a text from Aries.

"Aries needs me to meet him in the war room."

"War room? What war are you fighting?" She chuckled.

I was hesitant to tell her, but she needed to know. "Your father's books had encryptions and ciphers in them."

She gave me a sly smile. "Yes, I know. I'm the one who told you about them, remember?"

I let out a breath. "What's Daphne doing?"

"Probably working. Why? Orion, what's wrong? You're worrying me." Her brows pinched, and I could see her body tensed.

"This conversation won't be easy, little flame. It's best if all of us sit down and talk about it."

"Daphne too?"

I nodded. "She needs to decide what she wants to do. So yes."

Her face was full of panic.

I raised her chin so that she would meet my eyes. I kissed her. "It's about your father's death."

She swallowed hard and closed her eyes. "Alright. I'll get Daphne. But could we not meet in someplace called the war room?"

I smiled. "Of course. I'll get the guys and will meet you on the terrace. We can all have breakfast.

"Breakfast and talking about death. Not the most appetizing combination."

Even though her obvious apprehension, she could push through the hard stuff. She was always resilient like that.

"I'll see you in a little bit."

She nodded, and I left, texting Leo and Aries about meeting me on the terrace instead.

❧ ❧

I found Sophia and asked her to make sure breakfast was pastries and other things that weren't too heavy on the stomach, and by the time I made it to the terrace, Leo and Aries were already pouring their coffee.

Leo huffed out a breath. He didn't look happy. Aries and I had pretty much taken all of Andee's time yesterday, and I knew he could tell.

"I'm the last man standing, aren't I, you assholes?" His amber eyes almost burned through both Aries and me. "Which one of you did she spend the night with last night?" He glowered at both of us.

"Neither," I told him.

His shoulders relaxed a touch.

"She didn't want to spend it with either of us until you and she worked things out between you."

"Oh," he muttered as Andee and Daphne walked onto the balcony. Cassie was in her pram, sound asleep.

Andee walked the pram toward Leo, stood on her tiptoes, wrapped her arms around his neck and kissed him. He grabbed her ass and lifted her against him, kissing her.

Daphne cleared her throat, breaking them out of their moment. "Could you not? Geez!" Daphne's playful smile at Andee made me chuckle as Andee literally slid down Leo's body.

"Later," he rasped against her ear, and a bubbly laugh escaped her as he playfully smacked her ass, as she pushed Cassie's pram toward the table.

"She's a vampire," I'm convinced of it," Andee mutter hissed. "This girl never sleeps at night and is barely awake during the day," she said with a flustered sigh.

"Hence the reason I suggested a nanny," I reminded her.

"Yeah, yeah, where's the coffee?"

Leo raised a brow, "Is that okay for the baby?"

"My doctor says one cup a day is perfectly fine."

He didn't keep at it, though I could tell he wanted to. Andee got her coffee and food, and he pulled her next to him in one of the lounge chairs. I could see in his face, he had no intention of letting her go anytime soon.

Leo was the one who broke the news to Andee about Atlas. She sobbed against him, and he wrapped her in his arms and comforted her for hours. He sent out for her all her favorite foods, and the two sat and watched dumb movies for two days straight. The tension between them melted away, and It killed me to watch, but he was who she needed. None of us thought it would be more than that. Just a temporary break in the awkwardness since her twenty-first birthday.

"So, about my father," Andee's words hung in the air as she looked at each of us.

Aries rubbed his neck and gave an awkward smile. "Yes, well.."-

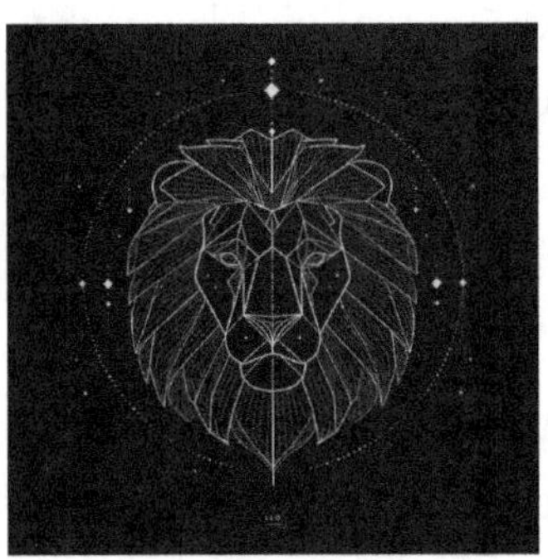

Leo

I was beyond pissed that Aries and Orion had been with Andee before me. It hurt more than I thought it would, but when Orion told me she hadn't spent the night with either of them, it made me feel a little less angry. I grabbed her perfect ass and her legs wrapped around me like they belonged there, and I wanted to take her into the closest room and shut the world out, having her all to myself. Daphne's voice broke our little bubble, but having Andee's body up against mine was like I was alive again. The light in my world was back. I pulled her into the nearest lounge chair and refused to let her go.

This was going to be a tough conversation. Aries had found something, not exactly what we were looking for, but hopefully it would lead us to it.

Aries cleared his throat. "We've been trying to crack Atlas' codebooks for a while. The cyphers and codes have been nearly impossible to figure out. We'd get close, and then hit a wall. Then Enzo Romano started buying up security firms out from underneath us, He's been patient, buying under shell corporations, and keeping the entire infrastructure, but implanting his own people in some of the upper management positions, and a few seats on boards here and there, never enough to prove what he was doing though."

"We've pretty much been running algorithm models non-stop for the past six months, in-between buying up security firms almost as quickly as Romano has," Orion added.

"Atlas' cyphers led me to an archived development server," Aries said. "I didn't know what to expect. I found partitioned environments labeled like astronomical phases like Orbit, Alignment, and Retrograde, but none of them formed a complete system. Atlas was building something that he was releasing in phases and distributing it to Romano." He cleared his throat. "Then this morning, there were anomalies in one of our systems, and we figured it out." He let out a defeated sigh. "Your father created a one-of-a-kind system of predictive models that can manipulate markets and supply chains."

Andee's breath caught.

I could see in Orion's eyes that he didn't want to scare her, but he knew sugarcoating it wasn't an option either. "This is the second breech on of our company's systems in a few months. But as far as a direct attack against us.." He let out another breath. "They haven't made a move against us. Not since your father," he said sadly.

Her eyes filled with tears, and seeing her face, I could see a rush of different emotions flood through her.

"That kind of restraint doesn't make this any better; it just means there's something we're missing. And until we figure out what else he was involved in... we stay ready," I told her.

"That's how he's been one step ahead?" Daphne asked. "This software?"

Aries took a sip of his coffee, then shook his head. "Not entirely. While we have technological resources and networks, Romano's are mostly tangible. We can affect some of what he does, sure, but there are a lot of things we can't touch, and it works the other way around as well."

"So, basically, real world versus digital." Andee added.

I smiled. "Yes."

Aries nodded. "The predictive risk model was imbedded in the software of a few companies we were looking to acquire. They had signatures, or digital fingerprints that were close enough to our own programs. Same fragments, same structure, across completely unrelated systems, but they shouldn't have been there."

"And these companies just let you dig into their systems?" Andee balked.

Aries smirked. "Sometimes. Sometimes not," he said with a devious smile.

Andee rolled her eyes.

"The program isn't finished," I said. "And we haven't been able to access it all. There's more; something bigger here. Atlas left the ultimate puzzle," I said with a little huff.

We sat quietly for a few minutes. Andee's body relaxed a touch, and determination filled her eyes. But I could tell her brain was still spinning, and her emotions were changing by the second.

"Why would he do that? Put everyone in danger?"

I squeezed her hand. "I wish we knew, baby girl."

"You, out of everyone, knew he wasn't the same after your mom got sick," Orion said softly. "Pain and grief will make a man do things he wouldn't normally do."

"You said these mafia men have tangible resources all over the cities they run, right?" Daphne asked.

"Yes. Why?" Aries asked.

She raised a brow. "Like doctors, or maybe specialists?"

"That makes sense, actually," I said.

Daphne scoffed. "Yeah, I tend to do that," she rolled her eyes. "Not everyone always listens though," she said, looking between the three of us, and we all winced.

"Point taken," Orion said.

"Not an apology, but as close as I'm going to get, so I'll take it." She beamed at the three of us.

"Anyway," I said. "We have a lot to figure out, and being here is the safest for everyone."

"We need to figure this out sooner rather than later." Andee's eyes flicked to where Cassie was. Aries had taken her out of her pram and looked literally enthralled with her.

"We will, baby girl," I said, pulling her close and kissing her like I was sealing a promise. Because I would give up everything for them.

Aries grasped Cassie's pram and told Andee that she needed a tour of the grounds. She rolled her eyes at his very obvious reasoning as I grasped her hand and led her inside, up the stairs and into my room.

I pulled her into my arms; the little sigh as she melted against me made my heart soar. I kissed the top of her head. "You were always ours, and we fucked up. We won't make the same mistake ever again. I promise," I lifted her chin so she was looking at me. "No one will harm you or Cassie."

She nodded. "I want to help."

I raised a brow. "We'll see," I said with a little chuckle.

Her brows narrowed, "I can be pretty persuasive when I want to be ya know."

I chuckled. "Oh, believe me, I know."

"All kidding aside, Leo. I want to help. This impacts me as well. I don't just want to sit around and do nothing." She let out a little sigh. "I understand why you guys didn't ask me to help before, and while I appreciate it, I need to do this."

I nodded. "I get that."

She kissed me. "Thank you."

Her breath hitched when I unbuttoned her shirt and fumbled with the buttons on mine. I unhooked her bra and laid her on the bed, pulled down her shorts and dragged her panties down with my teeth. Her little shudder sounds went straight to my cock as I kissed the inside of her thighs, and then the apex, and she murmured my name.

I hovered over her, kissing her nipples.

"That night, all I wanted to hear was my name on your lips as you fell apart under me," I confessed.

"I was so afraid Orion would end if I did," she said with a touch of nervousness.

"Orion's rules or not, a pack of wild horses couldn't have stopped me that night, baby girl."

Her hand wrapped around the back of my neck as she pulled me toward her, kissing me like I would disappear if she didn't. She reached for the button on my jeans, and a smile arched my lips.

"Such an impatient little thing, aren't you?" I teased as I slid out of my jeans and boxers, scooting her higher on the bed so I could lie next to her. She licked her lips, her hand barely touching the tip of my cock as I murmured her name. She straddled me and sank down almost painfully slow until she was fully seated and my cock was inside her tight, perfect little pussy. Her hips rolled as I touched her nipples, and she moaned my name like a prayer as I started to slowly lift my hips up and down, her pussy clenching my cock, making me hiss.

"Look at you, riding my cock like a good girl," I rasped, pulling her toward me and flipping her over. She squeaked as I did so, and I fucked her hard and deep.

"Yes, Leo! Fuck!" She screamed. "Harder, please!"

I sucked on her nipples and she writhed under me, her legs wrapping around my hips, pulling me closer, and with each thrust, her pussy clenched my cock like a vice, and a feral growl escaped my chest as her legs shook.

"I want you to come now!" I roared as I felt her pussy flutter around me, spurring my own release.

My name left her lips in a soft hiss, and it was the best thing I'd ever heard.

Once we had cleaned up, I pulled her against me, her crystal blue eyes not leaving mine. "You are the fire in my veins, baby girl, the danger I crave, and the weakness I can't resist. Every heartbeat for the longest time told me that loving you was forbidden. But you were a part of me, a part I can't live without. I love you."

"I love you too, Leo."

I was wrong. *That* was the best thing I'd ever heard in my life.

Andee

The revelations about my father had shaken me. My emotions were a jumbled mess, but more than anything, I wanted answers and the chance to fix whatever my father had set in motion. But I also knew it would take time, so I tried to enjoy the morning sun warming my skin as I sat on the terrace. Cassie was asleep in her stroller, and I was ordering the things I needed. First thing on the list: new undergarments. The guys could tell me all they wanted that my maternity bras were no big deal, and while I believed them, I needed something different. So the lacy black, white, and pink maternity bras were the first thing in the cart. Second thing: new panties. It had been over a month since we came here, and they had ripped or shredded seventy percent of my panties.

"Are you crazy!" I heard a woman scream. I rolled my eyes. The woman was here to interview for the position of nanny. This was the tenth this week, or was it the eleventh? The first one was so intimidated by Orion's presence alone that she dashed out of the villa, her resume literally floating in the air behind her. The second and third I got rid of because no matter how much I knew the guys loved me and would never even think of looking at another woman, they were hotter than hell. Aries teased me about it for days.

I watched the latest woman storm out, her hands moving around her wildly, as she cursed Orion's name. He strolled onto the balcony, as if nothing had happened, checked on Cassie, and then scooped me up so I was sitting on his lap.

"What did you insist upon this time? A cavity search?" I smirked.

His brow raised, "No, she wasn't on board with the emergency evacuation drills that are clearly stated in the list of requirements for the position."

"Let me guess, she didn't read that part."

"Clearly."

"You're the one insisting on a nanny, Orion; you can't keep rejecting them, or Cassie will be a teenager before you find 'the perfect one.'"

His lips teased against my ear. "What makes you think she'll be our one and only, little flame?"

My entire body shuddered at his words. "She's two and a half months, Orion. I'm not having anymore kids until she's out of diapers, and even then..."-

He kissed me with such passion that I lost my entire train of thought.

I finally pulled out of his grasp, my breathing heavy. "No fair."

His sexy-as-fuck laugh made my pussy flutter. "Don't forget the fact that you denied two yourself," he said, bopping me on the nose.

"That was different," I said, crossing my arms over my chest. His gaze made me want to climb him right there and then.

He reached down my shorts, pushing my thighs apart, his fingers playing with my clit. "This is the only little pussy I want wrapped around my cock for the rest of my life." His fingers started pumping in and out as I grasped his forearm, my head lolling against his chest.

"That's my good girl, come for me, I want to taste your sweetness."

Holy Mother of God.

His magic fingers went between fucking me and barely touching my clit, and my orgasm shot through me like a wave crashing against a rock. The things these men made my body do bordered on insane. "Orion, fuck," I rasped against him.

He pulled his fingers out and stuck them in his mouth, his eyes closed, like he was savoring it. "So sweet, so perfect, like fucking ambrosia," he rasped against my ear.

The sound of a throat clearing had me almost jump out of my seat.

"Senior Kane," Sophia's voice cut through my haze. "There is a woman here to see you from the agency."

"Ahh, my three O'clock is a little early. Thank you, Sophia." He kissed me, smiling deviously. He knew he was leaving me a puddled mess. The only consolation I got was seeing how hard I made him. So I gave him a satisfied smile and started scrolling on my laptop.

"Try to get this one's name before she runs out the door," I said as I tried to catch my breath.

His laugh echoed around me as he followed Sophia into the villa.

⟫⟫⟫ ⟪⟪⟪

It took two more weeks and ten more interviews before Orion and I decided on the right nanny for Cassie. Her name is Elena, and she had been the nanny for several children of high-ranking military figures over her career, so she knew all about escape protocols and every other crazy thing Orion and the guys insisted on. Plus, she was married to a lovely woman named Isabella. So all the boxes were checked.

It had been a month, and I still insisted on Cassie sleeping in my room, though I was spending most nights with one of them in my bed. I insisted they come to me for the first couple of weeks, but over time, all three decided they were tired of moving around. A crew came in and within two days, the walls surrounding all the bedrooms were gone, creating a suite larger than the apartment I had in the city. A man named Gerard came and redecorated, making it the perfect combination of all four of our styles. Cassie had her own little mini-nursery on one side, with a partition that could be slid open or closed. The guys wanted to ease me into having her in another room, and this way, Elena had access to her if I needed her to take over.

We got into a routine, but between them running their company, the meetings they had to be a part of, and figuring out what the Romano's had access to, it was a lot.

Leo walked onto the patio, scooping me into his arms, so I was sitting between his powerful thighs. He raised a brow at the book I was reading, and I pulled it to my chest, and he wiggled his brows.

"And just what kind of book are you reading, baby girl?"

"Romance," I said, trying not to gulp.

His eyes smoldered, and I felt goosebumps skate over my arms. His hand moved under my sarong and glided up my leg, his eyes full of mischief and promise.

Just as he touched my bikini bottoms, Aries cleared his throat.

"This isn't over, baby girl," Leo said with a devious look.

"What's not over?" Aries asked, sliding onto the chair next to me.

Leo snatched the book out of my hands and tossed it to Aries, despite my trying to get it back. I felt my cheeks get warm as Aries read a scene that was especially spicy.

Aries' eyes met mine, and then the two exchanged a look. A look of both promise and my ruin. Aries closed the book and tossed it onto the little table between the chairs. He put his arms behind his head and leaned back. "Well, I guess this means we'll be trying some new things while we're in Deià." He wiggled his brows.

"Where are we going?"

"A private spa called Luz de Mar, in Deià, on the coast. We are meeting some clients there on business, but are also using it as an excuse to whisk you away."

"For how long?" I was nervous about leaving Cassie.

Leo gently grasped my chin, so I was looking at him. "Just two nights," he said, kissing my nose. "Cassie will be fine," he said in a reassuring tone.

I let out a breath. I could do this. At least that's what I told myself.

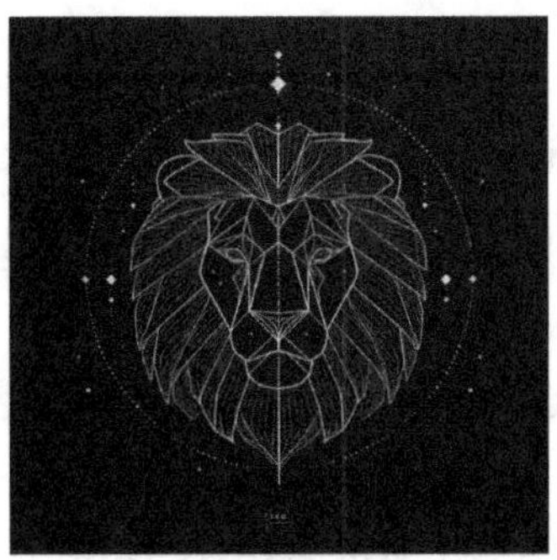

Leo

The jet ride to Deià didn't take long, and it was more than needed. We all needed a break from the situation with the Romanos. Andee looked like a goddess. She slipped her hand into mine as we took the stairs out of the jet. We arrived in Deià at sunset, and the sky welcomed us with a beautiful display of orange, pink, and yellow. The last of the light reflected off Andee's golden hair as the driver opened the car door.

Luz de Mar Spa sits carved into the cliffs above Deià, hidden between stone and sea like it was never meant to be found. Terraces of pale limestone step down toward the Mediterranean, each level softened with wild greenery, olive trees, lavender, and trailing vines that catch the salt air. Glass walls reflect the sky so completely, the structure almost disappears at certain angles, leaving only the sound of the water, quiet pools, slow fountains, and distant crash of waves.

Everything about it is deliberate. Private. Controlled. A perfect place for us to spoil our girl without the world nosing into our business. Not that I gave a fuck what others thought about our dynamic, but we didn't want to share her with the world; we wanted her all to ourselves.

We followed the valet to our private bungalow that sat slightly removed from the main terraces, tucked behind a line of cypress and stone, overlooking a narrow stretch of coastline far below. It's small but impossibly refined: whitewashed walls, dark wood beams, floor-to-ceiling glass that opens fully to the sea. Inside, luxury and elegance surrounded us with dark wood, whitewashed walls, and a center living space with a bed big enough for all four of us tucked into one of the corners.

Andee's mouth hung open as she walked in, spinning in a circle. Her bright blue eyes sparkled when she saw the bed, and I noticed her cheeks bloomed pink. I couldn't help but smile.

"Where would you like the suitcases, sir?" the valet asked Orion.

"Just leave them over there," Orion said, pointing near the wall.

"Very good, sir. Is there anything else I can do for you?"

"Not right now, thank you," Orion said, slipping a tip into the man's hand.

The man nodded and took his leave.

"This place is insane." Andee cried out with pure wonder on her face.

I strode up to her, reaching around her tiny waist. "And there's a private pool in the back," I said, kissing her neck. Her soft moans went straight to my cock.

"I'll get changed," she purred. But I didn't let her go.

"Who said anything about changing?" I asked with a devious smile.

"What do you... oh!" Andee's face blushed. She was adorable. She was a little wildcat in the bedroom, but outside of it, she still blushed, and I loved it.

I scooped her up as Orion slid open the glass door that led to the private pool and cove in the back. Golden light shone from little lights, reflecting on the clear water, its edges blending seamlessly with the horizon beyond, as if it spilled into the sea. Beyond the pool, a set of worn steps led down to the entrance of the hidden cove, narrow, secluded, and completely shielded by the cliffs that rose on either side.

I set Andee down gently and kissed her neck as Orion slowly untied her sundress, the material pooling at her feet. Aries knelt, kissing her thighs as he slipped her little pink panties down, and I unhooked her bra, letting her perfect tits free from the lace. I gently touched one of her nipples, and her head lolled against my shoulder. I guided her to a large daybed, and she sat up on her elbows as she watched us undress, licking her pink lips, her eyes full of desire.

"I can practically smell your arousal, kitten," Aries murmured as he crawled over the perfect curves of her body. He kissed her nipples and neck as Orion and I lay on either side of her. She reached for Aries' cock; Orion and I reached for her hands, placing them above her head.

"No touching until we tell you, baby girl," I rasped in her ear.

She moaned incoherently as Aries planted himself between her luscious thighs. Her hips writhed as he fucked her with his tongue, and Orion and I put all our attention on her nipples. Her hips moved, seeking more as Aries teased her, and she moaned his name like a prayer.

"Such a good girl," I rasped in her ear. "Look at you getting fucked, you're perfect."

She moaned out Aries' name as he sucked her clit so hard her entire body shattered.

Aries rose from between her thighs and kissed her. "Fucking ambrosia," he rasped.

Orion's eyes met hers. "We're going to try something different tonight, little flame." Her breath caught as he caressed her nipple. "I want you to straddle Leo," he told her.

She did as he asked and let out the sexiest sound as her pussy sank down my cock. Orion touched her ass, and she moaned as he caressed her.

"We're filling all your holes tonight, kitten," Aries said with a devious smile.

Her pupils dilated, and I smiled. "I think she likes the idea."

Orion pressed his finger near her hole, and she shivered. "Do you like that idea, little flame?"

My hips moved slightly, and her lip caught between her teeth. "Yes, Daddy," she purred.

"Good girl," Orion rasped.

He grabbed a bottle of lube and ran his hand over his cock as he breached Andee's puckered hole. She let out a soft cry, and Aries caressed her cheek while I slowly continued to move my hips.

"Shh," Aries murmured. "Breathe and let him in."

She closed her eyes and nodded as Orion pressed deeper inside her. Aries raised her chin and pressed his cock against her lips. "Open for me, kitten, I'm going to fuck this beautiful mouth." Orion hissed as he moved his hips. "So tight, fuck," he rasped. The two of us moved opposite each other, and I pinched Andee's nipples as she moaned around Aries' cock.

Aries hissed and praised her as she licked the underside of his cock, and then he pumped his hips slowly.

"Fuck, look at you," Orion rasped as he fucked her ass. "Such a good toy for us."

She let out a quiet mewl sound around Aries' cock as Orion pinched her clit and she exploded, her body writhed, clenching my cock like a vice and I growled her name as my cum filled her pussy. Aries and Orion found their release, and Andee collapsed on top of me.

"Holy fuck," she breathed. "That was just...holy fuck."

I chuckled as we separated, and Orion lifted her, taking her to the shower. Aries and I followed. Once we were cleaned up, I wrapped Andee in a fluffy white robe and guided her into the giant bed. She crawled into the middle, and we all surrounded her. I was behind her, Orion in front, and Aries above her. We always moved around when we were at the villa, each of us taking turns holding her while she slept. I didn't care where I was, as long as I could touch her, I was content.

Her breathing evened out, and the three of us shared a look. None of us had to say the words. We all knew we were the luckiest men in the world.

Orion

The Mediterranean stretched endlessly in front of us. The meeting we had with a client went well, but the hour we were in the room felt more like three. Andee planned to meet us on the terrace overlooking the sea. She was standing with her back to us, and even from the distance we were at; she was stunning. Her golden hair flowed over her shoulders, and her white gauze sundress made her skin look like it was glowing. Then the hair pricked up on my neck. A young man was casually leaning against the railing. Not next to her, but close enough to draw a growl from me. Her body stiffened and her hands grasped the railing as if she were going to fall.

Matteo DeLuca.

Andee's ex.

He shouldn't have been there. But it clicked in my head. Different last name. Different branch. Romano blood through his mother's side. Distant enough to stay invisible, close enough to be trusted, and completely outside anything we were tracking. He moved closer as we walked toward Andee. I didn't rush to her side like I wanted to. Like we all wanted to. But being as casual as possible, so as not to give anything away.

"Andee," he said, like it had been days, not years. Too casual and friendly. Too personal.

Too close, asshole.

I could feel the anger rising off Aries and Leo, and the tension and fear rolling off of Andee. Leo stood behind her, Aries to her right. I didn't move, but the air changed, sharp and cold. Matteo's eyes flicked between us. Fear. But then his fake persona re-surfaced. He took us in, measuring us, before his gaze settled back on her with an amused smile.

"I hear congratulations are in order," he added with a casual smile.

I was close enough to her to know her pulse spiked. Not because of what he said, but because of how he said it. Too calm. Too deliberate. The bastard knew exactly what he was doing.

"I'm not here to cause problems," Matteo continued, his hands in mock surrender.

Aries let out a quiet, humorless laugh. "That's comforting," he said drolly.

Matteo smiled faintly, but his eyes never left Andee. "I just wanted to see you," he said. "Make sure you're...doing okay."

Silence thick enough to be sliced filled the air. That's when I stepped forward, not between them, but nearly. Close enough that Andee felt the shift in control immediately, because her grasp on my jacket loosened just a touch.

"Careful," I said quietly

The little fucker didn't back down.

"I wouldn't be here if I didn't care about you," he said, only looking at her. Almost like he meant it.

But there it was. Not a threat. Not directly. But a message. He knew. Not just about her, but about the baby. And if he knew, so did the Romanos.

The three of us closed around her without a word. A wall. A warning.

I wanted to smack the smug smile off his fucking face. "Really, Andee, I just wanted to make sure you're okay with the decision you've made," Matteo said softly. "Who you choose to stand with has a way of making things...easier." Then he looked right at me. "Or a lot more complicated."

He smiled like the cat that ate the canary, and then he turned, walking away like he didn't just change everything. They found her here. And they could do it again.

Once he was gone, she crumpled into my arms. "Take me home, please, Orion."

I kissed her forehead. "Of course, little flame."

She sat curled in Leo's lap as Aries and I packed up the suitcases, and she refused to let him go when the car arrived. She was in shock. I don't know what that little asshole did to her in the past, but if he ever tried coming near her again, I would end him. Fuck who his relatives are. Thankfully, she fell asleep on the plane, still curled up in Leo's lap.

I was a ball of emotions. Raging because he was near her, mad at myself because I didn't look into the connection between Matteo and Romano.

"I don't know what he said to her that day at the coffee shop, but she was terrified," Aries growled low.

"She never mentioned him after they broke up," Leo murmured.

None of us spoke for a few minutes.

I let out a breath and rested my head against the seat. My rage was still simmering, but my guilt was bubbling up.

"This isn't all on you. Why would we have looked into her ex?" Aries asked.

We'd known each other long enough that we sometimes joked that we shared a brain. Aries knew I was thinking about how I could have missed that her ex was related to Romano.

"He clearly hasn't been associated with them until recently, or he would have come up in the threat assessment," Leo whispered.

I nodded. "Yeah," I rumbled low. "I know."

He was right, but I still felt like I had failed her. *Again.*

Andee

Once we returned from the spa, I was shaken, for certain. Seeing Matteo terrified me. He found me and knew about Cassie. If the guys hadn't been anchoring me, I don't know what would have happened.

The next morning I was on the terrace with the guys when Orion's eyes met mine. "You never told us what he did, little flame." There was concern and hurt in his eyes.

I swallowed hard; it was time to rip the bandage off. "We broke up because he proposed right before Mom died."

All three of them stopped what they were doing. "You never said anything about that," Orion said with a touch of roughness in his voice.

I shook my head. "I didn't want to think about it, or him. I was focused on Mom," I said with a touch of sadness in my voice. "Then, I didn't hear from him until a year later, and I just thought he was crazy," I admitted. "The day in the coffee shop, he was acting all weird and possessive, like he was expecting me to fall at his feet and get back together."

"Clearly, he was," Aries said with a huff of a laugh.

"He's related to Romano, isn't he?" I murmured.

Orion raised my chin, so I was looking at him. "No one will touch you. Ever."

He kissed me, sealing his words as a promise. I sighed and snuggled closer, taking in his scent that was just…Orion. It made me feel lighter, and I nestled against his chest and felt like I could breathe again.

After taking a swim and putting Cassie down for her nap, I was restless. I walked into the computer room. Orion, Leo, and Aries were all hovered over different computers, all engrossed in their work. Exchanging pieces of paper with formulas scrawled over each with red and green check marks. I plopped into one of the chairs and kicked my feet up on the desk. I was bored out of my skull. Elena was watching over the baby, and I was trying my best to let her do her job. It wasn't easy. I never had a nanny, so it was weird for me to get used to the concept.

I sat by Aries' work area, and his eyes were on me. "What?" I asked.

"Nothing," he smiled.

"Trouble," I murmured, and he gave me the smallest of winks, but it still made me shiver.

Leo's brow was furrowed, and he cursed, slammed his fist against the desk, and pushed his chair away, his hand running through his blond hair. He saw me, smiled, and pulled me onto his lap. "Good. I needed a reason to take a break," he said, kissing me, making me weak in the knees.

"Hey! I'm here to help," I half teased.

Leo chuckled. "And you are helping,"

I balked. "Ha ha."

I stared at the screen; it was full of code, all blinking different colors, a jumble of numbers and letters that seemed meaningless. I hopped off Leo's lap and pulled a chair in front of the screen. My fingers hovered, then instinctually, as if I were in a trance or something, I traced the sequence, aligning it with the subtle patterns of dates, initials and sequences my father had scattered in puzzles and games he had given me to solve my entire life. One by one, the symbols clicked, rearranging themselves into a coherent pass phrase. The screen blinked green, and a single folder appeared.

"Atlas Sentinel?" Orion's deep, raspy voice wrapped around me, and I realized all three of them were standing close, watching the screen. "What the fuck is Atlas Sentinel?" He rumbled.

"I have no idea why are you asking me?" Aries huffed with an exaggerated expression.

"I wasn't asking you, I was just.." –Orion shook his head. "Never mind. We need to figure what this is."

"Well, staring at the thing won't do us any good," Leo said, gesturing for me to click on the folder.

I jumped up from the chair, shaking my head. "Oh no, I will not be the one to open Pandora's box," I said, bumping into Aries' chest. His grip around my waist made my heart flutter.

His lips brushed against my ear. "'You're the one who cracked it, kitten; you get to open it."

I looked between the three of them. "Okay, but I will not be to blame if all the computers blow up."

A small smile arched Orion's lips. "Noted, little flame."

I walked toward the keyboard, my hand hovering, almost shaking, as I clicked on the folder. Hundreds of folders popped up on the screen. Then a video started, one that made my knees nearly collapse out from under me. Orion's powerful arms held me up as I stared into the face of my father. He was older than I remembered. Not physically, but in his eyes.

"My dearest little star," he started, and I almost broke. Orion pulled me onto his lap, holding me, grounding me, as my world felt like it was going to collapse around me.

Aries

I watched the face of a man I respected, who I had known my entire life, look broken and tired, but determined. Andee nearly collapsed from just seeing his face on the screen; Orion caught her. Then, when Atlas started the video by calling her his little star, Orion scooped her up in his protective embrace as we watched.

"You and your mother were the most important things in my entire life. When she got sick, I did things I wasn't proud of. I developed a predictive model not for power, but for leverage. When your mother's treatments turned to experimental, the cost rose higher each day. I was afraid I would lose her, but in my selfishness, I also feared my financial ruin."

"Fucker," Leo murmured so quietly, only I heard him, thankfully. Andee was engrossed in the video. I gave him a look, and he challenged, but relented, as we both turned back to the screen.

"I needed certainty, contracts that couldn't collapse, markets that wouldn't shift unexpectedly, partnerships that wouldn't betray me mid-negotiation. I build small forecasting tools to protect income streams. Then larger ones to anticipate regulatory movement. I never meant to build something that became so vast."

Orion's fingers drew circles on Andee's back. "Do you want to take a break?"

She shook her head. "No. I want to hear this. I want to hear him explain it." Her voice was tense, but not in a sad way. There was fire in her eyes.

Atlas' voice changed.

"The potential was too great not to continue, but for that, I needed revenue." The guilt was clear in his voice. "But the program worked too well, and the Romano's wanted more. They saw the predictive advantage, but when I tried to kill the program, they interpreted as a breech in our agreement. They gave me one choice: finish or else. I refused to put you in danger, so I continued."

"What started out as something small turned into something that could change the world. I built a system that doesn't just predict outcomes; it learns from them, adapts, and influences the conditions that create them."

Atlas let out a sigh. "I'm so sorry, little star. I apologize for building it, for underestimating what men like Romano would do with something like this. Desperation is a powerful weapon, and they knew how to use it. But I was determined to stop them. There are documents in a folder named Andromeda. The documents give you full access to the program, outline the trust structure, the consolidation clause, and contingency triggers. I did what I could to keep you as safe as possible."

"I knew Orion, Aries, and Leo would protect you not because they were loyal to me, but because I know they love you, little star. On your twenty-first birthday, the cameras in the sitting room were live. Orion, Aries, and Leo all looked at you the same way I looked at your mother the first time I laid eyes on her. I could see their love for you in the purest form. Their eyes told me it was the way things should be. The world can overwhelm any of you. It will never overwhelm all of you."

"Again, my little star, I am so sorry. I love you, Andromeda."

The video ended, and Orion wiped the tears away from Andee's cheeks.

"Do you want me to click on the folder, kitten?" I asked softly.

She nodded.

If I thought I was furious before, after reading the documents, I was enraged by what Atlas had done.

Andee's voice cracked. "What the fuck was wrong with him? How could he do this?"

She practically leapt out of Orion's lap, her hands shaking with rage. He had not only put everything on her shoulders, legally, but he had guaranteed one of us would have to marry her. I didn't know if he did it that way because he didn't want all of us to have her, or what, but it didn't just complicate things; the way she looked at the three of us, it broke her. She knew what it meant, and she dashed out of the room.

Leo picked up his phone, "Daphne, she's going to need you. We found a video from her father."

Even without being on speaker, I heard Daphne's curse.

Leo ended the call.

"Now what?" I asked the others.

Orion ran his hand through his hair. "We have to figure out a way to stop it. Who knows what just opening the document triggered. If there are already systems in place, fragments of this code he let the fucking Romano's have, fuck only knows what they'll do."

I blew out a breath, "If it was worth killing him for... it should've been worth coming after us too. That they haven't means they're weaker than they are letting on."

"We'll have to figure all that out," Orion said.

"I watched her with that code. She doesn't look at screens the way we do. Orion sees structure; I see movement, where the pressure builds and where it breaks, and Aries, you see vectors and implementation. Andee saw the sequence. She watched the data cascade, and her eyes didn't track numbers; they tracked patterns. Patterns Atlas taught her. We need her to work with us to figure this out," Leo said.

"We also need to use our own beta model to understand how to stop this thing. Something that will allow us to watch actual data, without fucking things up," I noted.

"A mirror program would work," Leo said.

"Will that put too much pressure on the system?" I asked.

Leo shook his head. "Live global inputs will be used in the mirror system, but won't let anything execute."

"And what about the Romanos?" Orion asked.

"We can implement systems that have no effect on global markets or government agencies, accessing systems to analyze only their systems."

"That won't make them happy," Orion said.

We always knew the Romanos' strength was in the real world—their connections, their reach, the influence that kept them a step ahead of us in buying up security firms. What we didn't know was what they had access to in the digital world. Atlas had been working with them; we'd known that for years; but whatever access they'd been given never triggered a single red flag. No anomalies, no breaches, nothing that suggested they were building something beyond what we could already see. Until now. The video changed everything. Whatever Atlas gave them, whatever they'd quietly had access to all this time, it wasn't incomplete or harmless. It was deliberate, buried deep enough to go unnoticed, hidden well enough that even we missed it—until it was already too late to ignore.

"He recorded that video here." Leo whispered. "He was doing a lot behind our backs. That video wasn't from five years ago."

We all missed the change in Atlas. The video showed a man who was hiding something. I could see the evasiveness in his eyes and the way he moved when he spoke. We were all blinded by our own shit and didn't press enough to check on our friend, and I felt like an asshole because of it.

Leo checked on Andee once the mirror build was complete, as Orion and I pulled an all-nighter digging as deeply as we could into the program without triggering anything, Problem was, we had no idea if we already had.

Orion stretched, leaning back in his chair. The clock screamed at us; it was six A.M.

"What's the matter, old man? Can't handle an all nighter anymore?" I teased, and Orion flipped me off.

"You're only two years younger, asshole," he rumbled, but there was a teasing tone to his words.

"This shit is like nothing I've ever seen. It's a roadmap, not of streets or satellites, but of patterns. Financial flows, corporate structures, enforcement timing, commodity shifts, regulatory pressure, the invisible threads that decide who falls and who survives before anyone knows a move has been made."

Orion nodded. "Atlas didn't create something that hacks governments. He created something that predicts reactions. It doesn't break into systems; it models behavior so precisely that it's undetectable until it isn't. It's learning even as I move through this program."

I blew out a breath, "He really fucked us all over. That whole thing about us loving her, all of us, do you think he did this on purpose?"

Orion nodded. "He understood it, but that didn't mean he approved of it. No one could have predicted the chain of events."

The realization that it would be Orion marrying Andee made me more jealous than I'd ever been. They had a daughter together, for fuck's sake.

Orion turned his chair, looking at me. "It's a piece of paper. It means nothing, changes nothing."

"That doesn't change the fact that in public she will be the one on your arm." The bite in my words, I could tell, weighed on Orion.

"I didn't do this on purpose," he said with a little more force than I think he intended.

I shook my head. "I know. I'm sorry. This is a lot all at one time."

"It is. We have to make sure she doesn't get put in the middle anymore than Atlas has already done. Make sure she doesn't feel trapped."

"Meaning?"

"Meaning, we discuss this as a group: what she wants to do, what's best for everyone."

I cracked a smile. "How very modern of you," I laughed.

I got a rumbling noise in return.

"We should go check on Andee," Orion said. "Set the mirror build, and we can go."

I nodded, clicking on the program Leo had set up.

And because fate has a fucked up sense of humor, Orion's phone rang. We both looked at it like it were a bomb about to explode. And we weren't too far off.

Orion

My phone rang from an unknown number. Somehow, after everything we'd just learned, we had no idea the phone call I was about to answer would put our lives on a path that tied our hands.

We had been working on cracking Atlas' code for months. It took Andee less than five minutes. She was sixteen when I discovered just how much like Atlas she was. I knew she'd been getting into things she shouldn't have since she was ten, but as she got older, she became more bold, as if chasing some kind of rush. She had somehow hacked into a private financial server that Atlas had explicitly forbidden anyone to touch. I caught her fingers frozen over the keyboard, a mixture of exhilaration and fear in her eyes.

"Andee," I said sharply, my voice low, and she looked at me with fire in her eyes, almost as a challenge. "Do you even understand what you're doing?"

She smirked, a little too proud, and shrugged. "I just wanted to see if I could, Orion." Like it was the most natural thing in the world. My chest tightened. She had talent and recklessness in equal measure. That day I realized she wasn't just curious; she was brilliant, audacious, and utterly unstoppable when she set her mind to something.

Andee saw something in those numbers that we didn't. We were trained to look for intent. She was raised to look for alignment. Atlas didn't teach her code; he taught her how he thought. Our dinner conversations about risk, about timing, and about human nature wrapped into business language. She absorbed all of it. Her mind works like his. Not because she memorized anything, but because her mind bends the same way. That's the difference. We trained to protect the board. She was raised understanding how it was built.

Atlas had done something that started out of desperation, and it got away from him. He put his daughter at risk, and the entire business, and I was more angry with him than I had ever been. But the man who created the Atlas Sentinel program was not the man we knew since we were kids. He looked tired but calm in the video. His apologies were genuine, but there was something else behind his eyes. Something that told me he was going through something he was hiding from us.

Months before his death, he pulled away from us. Even though he never worked for MI6, I know he worked as an interrogator through private companies, meaning he knew how to hide and mask feelings, breathing, and eye movement. I should have known there was something more to it, but the level of familiarity and trust between us was like having blinders on. I never saw it.

There had to be a way to stop the Atlas Sentinel program; we just had to find it. But my first priority was Andee, and of course, Cassie.

"Hello?" I said.

"Signore Kane?"

"Speaking."

"This is Signore Romano's assistant; he is requesting a meeting with you and your business partners."

"And what is this regarding?"

"He is inviting you and your business partners to meet at a location of your choosing the day after tomorrow."

"Regarding?"

"I am not at liberty to discuss it over the phone."

"Then we will have to decline Signore Romano's invitation."

"He asked me to have you check your email, signore. You can call me back at this number to let me know where you would like Signore Romano to meet you. Until then, good day."

I ended the call. The look on Aries' face was one of anger and concern as I clicked on the email.

The photo was grainy but unmistakable. Andee, eighteen, flushed and laughing at a summer gala. My hand was on her waist. Aries pressing a chaste kiss to her temple, Leo leaning close enough to suggest something intimate. Harmless gestures, taken out of context, weaponized perfectly.

The look on Aries' face was the same as I was feeling: guilt, anger, and the realization that they had been watching all of us for a long time.

"We need to meet with them," Aries said. "This is our fault, as much as Atlas'."

I nodded and pressed the redial button on the phone.

"Yes, Signore Kane?" The woman answered, her voice with a smug tone laced through her words.

"We will meet the day after tomorrow, five PM, Ashbourne & Co. in Mayfair."

"I will inform Signore Romano."

The line went dead.

I shot a text off to our ops team, telling them what we required before take-off. Including a new sweep of cameras, microphones, and surveillance tech on all the transportation we would use for the trip.

Aries looked at me. "They're safer here."

"I agree."

"She won't be happy about it."

"No, no, she will not."

The fire behind her eyes made my cock strain against my jeans. She was pissed.

"I don't want to hide, Orion!" She hissed out.

"Little flame," I said in a deep tone.

She crossed her arms over her perfect breasts. "Don't little flame me."

Aries stifled a chuckle.

Leo approached her carefully and touched her arm. She didn't flinch; she allowed him to pull her into his arms.

"You need to stay here, please," he said, raising her chin so she was looking at him. "I know it's not fair, but we don't know what they know, baby girl, and this place is the safest for you and Cassie."

She melted against him, and a streak of jealousy hit. But I know we are all here for her in our own ways. Even when she doesn't say it, we know what she needs. Leo gives her steadiness, the unwavering calm that holds her when her world threatens to topple. A quiet anchor, a shield against the chaos of the world. Aries brings fire, a spark that makes her laugh, makes her remember she's alive, reckless in all the ways the world wants her to forget. But when the storm hits hardest, I step in. I command her attention, her focus, her breath. She needs to be reminded that she's safe, that nothing outside these walls can reach her, not for a moment. And I always make sure she feels it in every fiber of her body until she's steady, until the fear shrinks away, until she remembers where she belongs.

"On one condition," she said, giving me a coy smile.

I raised a brow at her. "And what would that be, little flame?"

"When you get back, I want to know everything. And I want to help stop this program. Work with you all, not sit around here acting like some woman who can only make sure dinner is on the table when her man comes home."

I pulled her away from Leo, my lips brushing against her ear. "Oh, little flame, the only dinner we want on the table is you, laid out like a banquet before us."

She shivered in my arms, and then a coy smile arched her lips. My cock pressed against her.

She pulled out of my arms. "I need to check on Cassie," she said, sauntering into the villa. All three of us let out an audible groan as we watched her perfect hips and ass as she walked away. The three of us shared a look. None of us wanted to leave her, not even for a night.

The following morning, I found Elena in the nursery with the baby. "Have you seen Andee?"

She shook her head, "No, Senior Kane. She texted me this morning asking me to handle Cassie's morning routine."

I walked across the room and kissed my daughter. She was giving genuine smiles, and each time she smiled at me, my heart was lighter.

"Thank you, Elena."

She nodded, and I headed out the door.

I searched the villa and ultimately found her in the library. The only light was a soft glow coming from the desk light and I heard crying. I walked around the desk and found her with her knees pressed against her chest and her cheeks stained with tears.

I scooped her up and sat her with me on the velvet couch. "What's the matter, love?"

"Orion, he..he.." She laid against my chest and cried. That's when I noticed a journal sitting on the floor.

"Breathe," I murmured against her head, kissing her and smelling her scent of roses and rain. "Just breathe, little flame." I felt her head nod against my chest, and after a few shuddering breaths, she started explaining.

"The video was bothering me," she started. "I recognized the room he was in, and I found myself in here, searching for something, anything to explain why he did what he did. And I found it." She walked to the other side of the room and picked up the journal, handing it to me. Flipping to earlier dates, she stopped on one right after Maeve had been diagnosed.

August 5, 2023–Maeve is sick. I can't even say what she was diagnosed with, let alone write it down. She didn't tell us until I had to take her to the emergency room. But no matter what, I will fix this, whatever it takes.

Andee flipped a few pages ahead; this one dated a few months later.

January 2024–I'm close, closer than I've ever been, but proximity doesn't pay for time. They're offering access, resources, scale... more than enough to finish this. I don't trust them, but I'm running out of options and running out of time. And that is something I won't allow.

The next entry she flipped to was a few months after he was here with Maeve.

August 2024–It's moving faster than it should, patterns where there shouldn't be patterns. They keep asking for more, but it doesn't stop where they think it does... it doesn't stop. I won't finish it. I can't.

"Every entry, he sounded more and more like his mind was slipping, Orion." Her face fell. "Then there's the last one," she barely murmured.

The last entry was the week before Atlas was killed.

September *2025-I told them it doesn't stay contained. If I open it, if I let it out—no, they won't risk that. They can't afford what happens next.*

"He wasn't in his right mind, Orion," Andee cried out. "He was so lucid in the video; I don't understand how I didn't see it."

I reached for her, holding her against my chest. "This isn't on you, love. None of us saw it. Your father could always hide things and manipulate situations; that's what made him so good at his job. Your mother's illness broke him."

I drew circles on her back, just holding her until her breathing evened out. Then she looked at me, determination on her face. "I won't let them get away with this, Orion. I mean it."

I couldn't help the smile that pulled at my lips. "Oh, I believe you, little flame. How did you find the journal, anyway?" Another smile crossed my lips.

"The books are categorized by color and number patterns, and the journal didn't fit where it was on the shelf," she said like it were the most logical thing in the world.

"Of course it wasn't," I chucked.

She raised a brow at me, putting her hands on her beautiful, curvy hips.

"Are you teasing me, Orion Kane?"

I chuckled. "Absolutely not."

"I can tease too, "she said with a breathy tone. She straddled my lap and her eyes filling with desire as she moved her hips against my cock.

A low growl escaped from my chest. "Careful, little flame."

Before meeting with the Romanos, we called on a former MI6 operative and friend. One who still did undercover work part time because he was bored off his ass.

We met Roman Grayson at a pub not too far from the restaurant. It was full of locals enjoying a pint right after work. I felt Roman's presence as we walked in. Aries ordered three pints, and we sat down at the scratched up wooden table, the chairs streaking across the worn floor. We dispensed with the pleasantries and got down to business.

He lifted his cap and ran his hand through his hair after explaining what we could.

"I trust your judgement in not sharing what Atlas got you three into. He was a good man, but could be a selfish bastard." Roman's harsh tone wasn't something he usually let people see. He was always cool and collected, luring his marks into a false sense of security.

Roman's hand hovered over his glass before he spoke in a deliberate tone. "Them not going after you, after Atlas, feels like internal correction," he said. "Too much exposure, and now they're compensating. When families like that pull back, it's not to disappear; it's making sure the next move lands clean. It doesn't make them any less dangerous; their playbook just changed. They won't strike openly, not after your first meeting.." -

"So, if we push them too far.."-I said, my voice low and measured.

"It will escalate quickly. They have an advantage in your sandbox now, so they will go with that line as long as possible."

Leo pinched the bridge of his nose. "So pretty much what we figured," he said, blowing out a long breath.

We knew what the stakes would be when we dealt with the Romanos. But that wasn't the main reason we met with Roman; we just needed leverage, and he had it.

"And their weaknesses? We need to know they're exploitable before we consider options," I told Roman.

His gaze hardened. "Debt, political exposure, internal fractures. But they're fragile in all the wrong ways. Make them think you're complying. But you need to think differently. Physical weakness versus technical. You may need outside help."

I exhaled slowly. That meant alliances I hoped never to call on: the Bratva. They controlled things Romano believed he controlled. I had thought about the real world versus digital before, but now that Roman confirmed it, it became an avenue we'd have to walk down, sooner rather than later.

We continued our talk with Roman for another twenty minutes before we parted ways. Walking toward the restaurant, I wished we had more time to strategize, but the walk only took ten minutes. We stood to the side of the small building. For once it wasn't pissing rain like it usually did all fucking year round in London. A heavy weight settled in my chest; Aries clapped me on the shoulder.

"We need to remember who the fuck we are when we walk in there," Aries said.

Leo and I nodded.

It was time to light the match, and pray we wouldn't be the ones to burn.

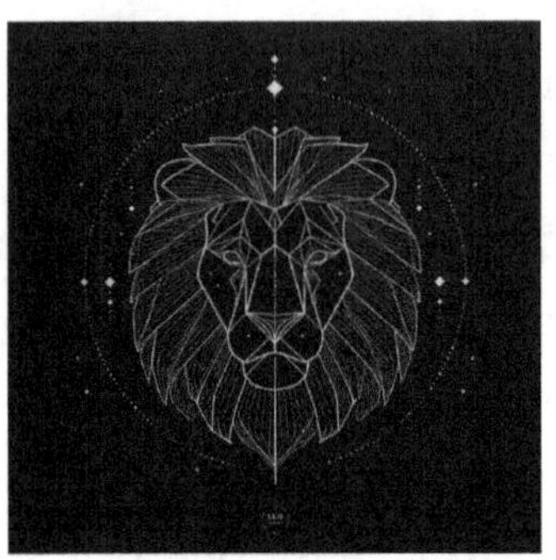

Leo

Leaving Andee was like leaving a literal part of me. I wanted to get back sooner rather than later. Orion checked in with both our ops team and security detail to make certain no one was watching, listening, or following us, and more importantly, no one was watching or listening to Andee at the villa. Having government officials as clients also made it easy for us to request a no-fly zone over the villa. They know we hold their contracts and deals, so it's mutually beneficial for both parties.

The meeting spot we chose was Ashbourne & Co. is a discreet, upscale private dining restaurant tucked on a quiet cobblestone street in Mayfair. The owners, May and Dale Ashbourne, were our very first clients. They put their trust and faith in us when they didn't have to. We were nobodies, and they treated us as if we were the most important businessmen in the world. We have always made sure that their business is secure, and they are more like family than anything.

We walked into the main room of the place; polished wood, soft golden lighting, and velvet booths give it a luxurious yet shadowed feel. The back room is reserved for high-profile clientele, and it's the perfect place for tense negotiations and meetings that look ordinary to outsiders while hiding the stakes behind frosted, etched glass doors.

Even with the revelations from Roman, this was still dangerous. All the scandal, investigations, and financial ruin were nothing compared to the ultimate response from the Romano's; our lives. No matter how much they had "pulled back," they were still the mafia.

"The picture is really bad," I said, as we sat on the plane to London. I blew out a breath and ran my hand through my hair. "This is big enough on its own to ruin all of us, trigger investigations and all sorts of nightmares that will ruin us."

My friends, my chosen brothers, both nodded in agreement. We hadn't shown Andee the photo. We planned on it, but when Orion found her in the library with Atlas' journal, we didn't have it in us. She was already so upset that she was literally shaking.

"She knows it has to be Orion," I admitted. "We talked about it last night while you guys were working."

Orion's brow knitted. "You should have waited until we could all talk about it."

"She brought it up, asshole, not me. This is Andee we're talking about; it was literally right in front of her. She's not stupid. You two share a kid. In the eyes of the public, and the picture, the optics are what they are."

"You know I don't care about that," Orion rumbled.

"That's what I told her. It's not changing anything. And how we would walk away tomorrow if we had to for her, for them," I added.

Orion nodded. "I agree. I'll call Adam about drawing up the legal documents."

Aries' lips tipped into a smile. "And *you* get to tell her about that," he said with a chuckle. He flipped Aries off, and a few minutes later the steward informed us we were preparing for landing at the private airstrip in London.

⤞⤞⤞ ⤝⤝⤝

"Boys!" Dale exclaimed. He clapped each of us on the back, drawing us each into a side hug.

"So good to see you! The room is ready, per your specifications, Orion."

"Thank you, Dale."

"Of course. Always. Anything for you, you know that." He gave a little wink as we walked into the back room.

We didn't have to wait long for the Romanos. Dale led them into the room twenty seconds after five PM.

Enzo Romano could have been the blueprint for every single mafia movie ever made. Slick back hair, pinstripe suit, red tie, black overcoat on his shoulders and a diamond pinky ring to complete the look. Flanking him were two younger men who looked like Enzo, his sons, Dante and Anthony. Behind them were several brick wall like men who stood around the room as Enzo and his sons walked to the table. We refused to go to them, and I could tell Dante was bothered by it. But his father gave him a quick glance, and he schooled his face as one of the other men took Enzo's overcoat.

We shook hands, and all sat at the same time.

"Let's get down to business, shall we?" Orion said with a rasp.

"Where is your lovely associate? Andromeda Voss, isn't it?" Enzo's face showed no emotion. He was a man who could threaten with just his words, no weapons necessary.

"I'm uncertain what you mean?" Orion said cooly. "Andromeda sold her shares of Centari over a year ago."

"Ah, yes," Enzo said with a knowing smile. "Please forgive me. I must have been misinformed."

Enzo looked at each of us before he continued.

"As for your other holdings...Atlas Sentinel," Enzo said, his voice smooth, almost casual, but the edge underneath cut through the air like a blade. "We'd like to make you an offer; let us take it off your hands. Men like you don't belong in the world this software touches, and you understand as well as I do just how dangerous it could be. Just how easily it could compromise reputations, partnerships, and contracts that took decades to build. Its capabilities are extraordinary...and, if mishandled, highly questionable. One wrong step, one slip in control, and the consequences aren't just financial; they're personal, public, and permanent."

"The program isn't complete," Orion said with a calm that even made Dante flinch for a split second. Orion was just as formidable as Enzo, and we'd used similar tactics when we needed to, except the Romanos didn't just deal in digital; they dealt in things that were tangible. "The system blocked everyone," he continued, his eyes calculating, watching every minute flinch, eye shift, and change in heartbeat. "Not just you, not just us," Orion said. "And in order to do anything, we need to finish the program. Or it will be unstable. Which, of course, is something none of us want."

Before Enzo Romano walked into the room, he already knew we understood he had access to part of Atlas's system. Still, the faint twitch in his left eye gave something else away: he hadn't expected us to meet him like this. Not directly. Not without hesitation. He moved subtly, settling in like a man accustomed to being the one who dictated how things unfolded.

"You want to protect what you hold dear," he said evenly, his gaze moving between us. "It's always interesting to see what men choose to protect," He sat back, and a smile arched his lips as one of his men pushed the photo of us with Andee across the table. There was a brief pause before he added, almost casually, "Restraint is often mis-understood. It isn't kindness. It's discipline."

Orion didn't move, didn't lean back or shift under the weight of it. He held Enzo's gaze without flinching. "Understood," he said calmly. "Just don't mistake our restraint for hesitation."

Something flickered across Enzo's expression, subtle but there. Gone as quickly as it appeared, replaced by a faint curve of his lips that didn't quite reach his eyes. "You speak as if that distinction changes anything," he replied. "You understand the position you're in, the exposure, the variables you can't control."

Orion's voice remained level, but there was a sharper edge beneath it now. "We understand exactly how you handle what you consider liabilities," he said. "And we're very clear on how we handle threats to what's ours."

The silence that followed wasn't empty; it settled into the room with weight, deliberate and controlled, each side measuring the other, giving nothing away. Enzo studied Orion for a moment longer than necessary, like he were recalibrating something. When he spoke again, his tone was smooth, almost conversational.

"Then we're aligned in principle," he said. "We prefer clean outcomes. Predictable ones. Which is why we'll keep this simple." He didn't raise his voice, didn't need to. "You'll complete what was promised. You'll ensure it functions as intended, and in return..." He let the words hang just long enough to land. "Everything remains contained." It wasn't a threat, not outright, but it didn't need to be.

Orion didn't answer immediately, and that pause was just as deliberate. When he did, his tone was just as controlled. "You're assuming control you don't have," he said. "Be careful not to base your expectations on that."

There was a shift in Enzo. Not agreement, barely acknowledgement of what Orion said, and yet a flash of almost what looked like respect washed over him. But it was gone just as quickly as it had appeared.

"Three months, gentlemen," Enzo said as if Orion's words didn't hold any weight. This was a man used to getting what he wanted. He stood then, unhurried, his sons falling into place beside him as if the outcome had already been decided. Like the conversation ended because he allowed it to.

Enzo and his associates walked out, and I turned to the others. "They were testing us, waiting for us to give, and when we didn't, they simply recalculated."

Both men nodded. We all understood they weren't backing down, but neither were we.

We strategized on the plane back to the villa. Each of us with a clear sense of what was needed to do.

"This is going to be a pressure campaign with them, and how far Enzo's restraint will allow him to keep from escalating," Aries noted. "He knew they fucked up, which tells me Atlas' death wasn't planned. But that doesn't mean he won't get to that point."

"I agree," Orion said, swirling his drink. "This is a different route for them, like Roman said. And they've had access to our digital world for a while, so we may need to delve into theirs, depending on how far this escalates."

"I suppose it isn't a bad idea. We just have to have something for them besides taking down the Romanos," I said.

Our plan to make the Romanos believe we were doing as they asked didn't put any of us in any less danger, but it would do what we needed, buy us time to get out of this, and until we knew what Atlas had built into that system, we weren't giving them an opening by moving too soon. So we would absorb it, control what we could, and keep Andee out of reach.

"Now, what about the elephant in the room?" I asked, cocking a brow.

"The wedding?" Orion said.

"Yes."

"She knows it's happening," I said.

Orion shook his head. "We know she knows."

I rolled my eyes at him. "But maybe it would be better for you two to talk about it?" I asked. "She needs reassurance, Orion. She doesn't want to hurt any of us by choosing."

Orion nodded. "I'll talk to her."

Did it kill me that he was the one who got to marry her? Yes. One million percent. But I was determined to keep my promise to her. Nothing would keep her belonging to all of us.

⤜⤜⤜⤜⤜   ⤛⤛⤛⤛⤛

It was late when we returned to the villa; the staff had already gone to bed. Soft music wafted from behind the dining-room door; we slowly made our way in. The sight before us made each of us audibly groan. Followed by possessive rumbles.

"So glad you're home. It was too late for dinner, but I figured it's never too late for dessert."

The sight before me nearly had me on my knees. Andee, sitting on the dining room table, wearing a deep blue pair of panties, a bra to match, along with thigh-high stockings and a garter belt, her luscious hair flowing around her shoulders, her sultry voice called to me like a fucking

siren's song. She was surrounded by champaign, strawberries and whipped cream.

"Well, gentlemen, you heard the lady." Orion rasped.

Andee

The night I discovered what my father had done nearly broke me. Daphne was waiting for me in my room. I collapsed in her arms, my body wracked with tears of anger, frustration, and betrayal.

Once the tears dried up, I explained what I could to Daphne.

"You're going to have to marry one of them?"

I nodded. "Of all the things that I found out, that was something I'd never thought about."

She raised a brow at me. "*Never*? Not even once?"

I let out a sigh. "Fine. Maybe once."

"I don't believe it was only once, miss.'I fell for them at fourteen.' What are you going to do?"

I shrugged. "I have no clue. How do I choose between them, Daph?"

She raised a brow.

"If you keep doing that, it's going to get stuck like that."

She stuck her tongue out at me. "Stop saying stupid shit, and I wouldn't have to."

"What do you mean?"

She pointed to the bassinet. "Fuck." The word stuck in my throat.

"Like Mr. Neanderthal would let you marry anyone else. You share a kid."

I shook my head. "They told me it didn't matter."

"In the eyes of the public, it will matter *a lot.*"

Sleep didn't come easily, even though I was mentally exhausted. I felt someone in the bed. Leo's scent of cedar and leather wrapped around me as he pulled me against him, his front to my back.

"Can't sleep, baby girl?" He asked with a raspy, teasing voice, nuzzling against me.

He turned me to look at him. I felt tears in my eyes again.

My vision blurred as the tears stung my eyes. I didn't have to say anything; he already knew. He turned me to face him.

He raised my chin with his finger, kissing me. "Listen, It's a piece of paper. Do you seriously think Aries and I are going to worry about what words are written on a piece of paper?"

"What about out in public, Leo? Very few people accept what we're doing. And you guys have a reputation to uphold. You've worked too hard to throw it all away for.."-

He put his finger on my lips. "We are not throwing anything away, so don't think like that. We have always controlled the narrative, and this is no different. We will not let society dictate what is right for us."

My shoulders relaxed a little, and I blew out a breath. "I want to believe you, Leo. I really do. This is so fucked up, all of it. What the hell was he thinking?"

"He wasn't." Leo's tone changed. "I believe him when he said it was never his intent to let it get out of hand, but he never knew when to stop and take a step back. He was always looking for the next thing."

I laid my head against Leo's chest. He was always the one who helped my doubts fade. I turned to each of them for different things, and I didn't even realize it until recently, even more so since everything changed.

Leo was the one who told me that my father had died. Not standing there awkwardly in the doorway, not offering hollow words, but sitting with me on the kitchen floor when the world felt like it was swallowing me whole. He didn't tell me it would all be okay. He didn't promise things he couldn't control. He just stayed. For two days, never leaving me, watching all the dumb movies I wanted to watch, and eating junk food. I still feel that same quiet strength. He makes the chaos slow down. Makes my breathing even out.

Aries is different; he refuses to let me sink. When my emotions get the best of me, he always drags me back to the surface with laughter, with reckless smiles, and that spark in his eyes that makes me feel like I'm not broken. Whenever I look at his smile, my spark comes back, and I can't help but smile back. He grounds me differently than Leo, making me remember who I can be, not who I should be.

Then there's Orion.

When the storm inside me gets too loud, too sharp, too much, I don't even realize I'm turning toward him until I already have. He doesn't soothe me in the way Leo does, or distract me the way Aries does. His commanding presence pulls all of me toward him. My focus. My breath. My attention. When I spiral, he steps closer, his voice, low and firm, grounding me in something solid and unmovable. When his hand slides down to my waist, or he tilts my chin up so I have to look at him, his commanding presence steadies me more than comfort ever could. When I'm with him, the world narrows. It becomes just us.

I slipped out of bed and texted Elena, asking her to take care of Cassie for the morning, and I went searching. I didn't know what I was looking for, but I needed an explanation regarding my father. I thought about it all night, barely sleeping. I slipped into the library, realizing from the video that's where he recorded it. When I found his journal, I slid down the wall and pulled my arms against myself, almost wishing I hadn't gone searching. The more I read, the more I realized he wasn't well. He had been pushed past his limit, and wasn't able to pull himself out. I blamed myself for not noticing.

I didn't even realize Orion had stepped into the room. He picked me up and helped me through things, bringing logic into the situation that I had only been seeing with emotion.

The three men left for London to meet with the man my father was working with, Enzo Romano. I was worried about them, and I tried to distract myself. I took Cassie for several walks around the vast grounds of the villa and even took her down to the beach.

My brain didn't stop humming the entire time they were gone. I knew Leo told me nothing would change, and I prayed he was right. I couldn't handle not being with all of them, even in public; that would suck. Leo reminded me none of them cared what people thought, and while that was spot on for them, it still tugged at me. Hopefully, there won't be a lot of public appearances in our future.

Cassie was asleep, and I put her in the bassinet and let Elena know I was going to take a shower. While I was in there, an idea popped into my head. Something I'd never done before, but the thought thrilled me the more I thought about it. I asked Sophie to get me what I needed. I wanted to do something that would pull us out of this situation, at least for a little while.

Everything was prepared, and with every tick of the gigantic clock on the mantle in the formal dining room, my pulse seemed to increase. I was sitting on the dining room table in lingerie. An ensemble of a deep blue pair of panties, a bra to match, along with thigh–high stockings and a garter belt. I let my hair down, skimming my shoulders. I was surrounded by silver bowls of fresh strawberries and whipped cream.

The door opened, and they stood there, not moving. Three sets of eyes darkened as they took me in. My body shivered as I watched them watching me like lions stalking their prey, and I was more than happy to be their prey. My eyes ran up and down their strong, muscular bodies, and that all three were tented in front made me wet just thinking about it. But it also made me feel powerful as fuck.

"So glad you're home. It was too late for dinner, but I figured it's never too late for dessert."

"Well, gentlemen, you heard the lady." Orion rasped as the three stalked into the dining room. Aries locked the door behind him.

Orion's eyes skimmed my body as he reached past me, his arm brushing my shoulder as he reached for a straw-berry. He dipped it in the whipped cream and pressed it to my lips. I swirled my tongue around it, then took a bite. Three audible groans filled my ears, and I smiled.

Leo and Aries cleared the table behind me as Orion helped me lie down. His eyes never leaving me as he ran his fingers up my thigh, leaving goosebumps in their wake.

"Fuck me, I can smell your arousal, little flame," Orion said in that deep, velvety voice that made things happen to my body.

I bared myself to him, and he kissed the apex of my thighs, just stopping short of my pussy. I moaned his name as Aries swiped two fingers into the whipped cream and put them into my mouth. I sucked them clean, running my tongue over his fingers as Orion made quick work of my panties. I felt the cold metal against my skin before I saw it. The small silver blade skimmed up my thigh, and Orion's eyes were full of lust with a hint of danger that made my body shiver. I heard the fabric against the blade as Orion cut both sides of my panties, and they fell to the floor.

"Much better," Orion rumbled. "Such a messy little cunt," he rumbled as he swirled his tongue around my pussy. "So ready to be fucked like the little toy you are, aren't you?"

"Yes, Daddy," I barely murmured.

Leo grasped my wrists, tying them above my head with the scarf I had draped over the table, his eyes full of promise. "No touching until we tell you, understand, baby girl?"

"Yes," I moaned as he ran his fingers down my arms and unhooked my bra, allowing my breasts to spill out.

A rasp of lust from all three of them filled the room, and I watched Aries and Leo's cocks strain even harder against their pants as they watched Orion's fingers dip into the whipped cream, and drew a line with his finger down my body. His magical tongue followed the trail until he reached my pussy. His tongue slipped inside and I writhed against him.

"So sweet, little flame. I could eat you all day for the rest of my life and always hunger for more of you."

He continued to fuck me with his tongue, flicking my clit with the tip as both Aries and Leo spread whipped cream on my nipples, each sucking and licking them, making my pussy flutter. Orion's muffled laugh made me clench harder.

"Fuck.."-I breathed. "It's too much," I moaned.

"You will take it and take all of it," Orion growled as his tongue pumped in and out of my pussy as Leo and Aries went between licking my nipples and feeding me strawberries.

Aries kissed me; I got lost in the sensation when Orion sucked on my clit so hard my entire body shattered. His muffled growl against my pussy made my orgasm continue as wave after wave of pleasure crashed over me like waves crashing against a rock.

"Good girl," Orion rasped as he stood, kissing me, letting me taste myself. My pulse quickened when I heard him unbuckle his belt and his cock sprang free.

"I'm going to fuck this little cunt hard and deep, fill you with my cum so you remember who you belong to," Orion rasped.

"Fuck, yes, please daddy, fuck me." I pleaded as his thick cock breached my pussy; a satisfied hiss escaped his lips. As Aries' cock sprung free over my mouth and I licked the tip.

"That's it, sweetheart, take all of my cock inside your perfect little lips," Aries hissed as his hips moved slightly, fucking my mouth.

"Look at you," Leo rumbled. "Being used like a little toy for us, such a good little girl you are." His cock was out and I tried to reach for him, forgetting my wrists were tied.

"Please, Leo," I begged around Aries' cock.

A dark chuckle erupted out of Leo as my wrists were freed, and I reached out for Leo's hard cock, pumping my hand up and down the shaft and stroking the tip.

"Fuck.."-Leo hissed as his head tipped back and he closed his eyes.

Aries hissed as his hips moved faster in and out of my mouth. Tears filled my eyes as he hit the back of my throat. His hand stroked my throat, and my eyes widened, and I grasped his hand, putting more pressure on my throat.

"You little minx," Aries said, his eyes filling with more lust than before. "We need a safe word," he murmured." If you want us to stop, you're going to say,"-

"Stars," I barely breathed out.

"Good girl," he rasped as the pressure on my throat increased. The sensation of everything happening to me made my pussy clench around Orion, who let a loud, possessive growl escape his chest.

"I'm.. oh my god!" I screamed around Aries as my orgasm hit me at the same time I felt Orion's cock empty inside me, my name like a prayer on his lips. Aries' cum shot down my throat, and Leo's painted my chest.

The room was full of the sounds of heavy breathing as Orion pulled out, and all three men took turns kissing me like I was the most precious thing in the world, even though I had begged them to treat me like their little toy.

Leo wiped my chest with the scarf, and Orion slipped his suit jacket around me, lifting me from the table and carrying me against his chest, and we walked down a small corridor I'd never seen. He walked up some steps, and Aries opened a door leading to the hallway in front of the bedroom. Leo opened the bedroom door, and Orion carried me into the bathroom.

Leo removed my garter belt as Aries rolled down my stockings; my shoes had been removed during our 'dessert' session. I felt loved and treasured as Orion turned on the water in the shower. He removed his clothes, and all he said was, "In." But it was his commanding voice of promise that had me moving faster than I had thought I could move.

Leo and Aries walked out, both smiling, shaking their heads. My eyes captured Orion's, confusion filling me.

"We need to talk, little flame."

Orion

Andee's eyes filled with confusion when Aries and Leo left just the two of us in the shower. She looked up at me with those crystal blue eyes of hers, looking for answers.

"We need to talk, little flame," I said.

She nodded.

I turned her so that her back was to the spray of water. "Tip your head back."

She did, and water cascaded down her back as I put shampoo in the palm of my hand and washed her hair. Just the fact that this little goddess was standing with me made my cock press against her ass, and she mewled against me as I continued to wash her hair. This would be a lesson in restraint, I knew that for certain. Watching her come with her little pussy wrapped around my cock, her breathy moans, and her screaming out around Arie's cock, was the sexiest thing I'd ever seen. The little vixen had planned 'dessert' all on her own and, fuck, if I didn't want to push the other two out of the room and have her all to myself.

She belongs to all of us. I reminded myself.

After I rinsed her hair, I wrapped my arms around her slender waist.

"Is this about us getting married?" She asked quietly.

"It is."

"You're not playing fair, Orion," she said. Then a smile arched her lips as she turned her head to look at me. "You standing here with your cock against my ass is not conducive to me being of sound mind." Her bubbly laugh made my cock twitch, and she pushed her ass against me.

"Now who's not playing fair?" I rasped against her neck.

"I know this is the best for everyone," she sighed and turned to face me. "And I know it's just a piece of paper. But it doesn't feel that way. I don't want to choose between you all."

"And you won't have to," I assured her, kissing her gently. "There will be some events after the wedding that we will all have our 'role' to play, but once this is all over, I don't give a flying fuck who has their arm around your waist, as long as its one of us."

I did care. Deep down. The possessive asshole in me wanted her to just be with me twenty-four seven. But I'd never do that to her, or to them.

"How many events?"

"Only a gala or two."

She rolled her eyes. "Only, huh?"

Her eyes filled with the fire that made my soul burn. "Well, I won't marry you unless you ask me properly."

The little vixen. I couldn't help the smile that arched my lips as I went to my knees, looking up at her.

"Andromeda Voss, would you do me the honor of becoming my wife?"

She considered me for a second, tapping her finger against her plump, pink lips.

"I..- Holy mother of God!" She screamed as I raised her leg over my shoulder and ate her out like I needed air to breathe. Her arms grasped my shoulders as her hips moved as I nipped at her clit and started fucking her.

"Oh my god.. FUCKKKK!"

"I'm not letting you come until you say yes," I blurted, then went back to fucking her, my teeth grazing her clit. Her legs shook, and I wrapped my arms around her, steadying her as her breath went ragged.

"I...Fuckkkk! "Yes...- fuck yes, I will!"

I sucked on her clit hard and she exploded on my tongue. I lapped up every drop of her sweet release as her orgasm pulsed through her body, clenching around my tongue.

She nearly crumpled, out of breath and pink cheeked. "Holy mother of God..." she barely got the words out.

I stood and grasped her by the back of the neck, kissing her deeply, allowing myself a moment of being the possessive asshole I wanted to be with her. Andee Voss was like a drug I never wanted out of my veins. When she wasn't in my life, it felt like I couldn't take a full breath. She was the missing piece of my soul, and I was a fool to ignore it for so long.

Three weeks after my proposal, Andee and I were in my office with my lawyer, Adam. I talked to him a few weeks back; I could hear the tension rolling off him. He was just as pissed at Atlas as we were.

"I'm all for the big splashy wedding, Orion, and I know you guys are forcing them into your narrative. Do you think it's wise?"

"Enzo will see it as a sign of emotional decision making." I told Adam. "That I'm locking down my weakness. They will know per the documents we're filing publicly that Andee is my beneficiary, so they will think the prize even more valuable than before."

Adam was quiet for a minute, then he let out a sigh. "Do you want me to draw up a silver bullet?"

"I wish I could tell you no," I said with a deep exhale.

"She's worth it?"

"They're worth it," I corrected.

"Stashing things away for a rainy day for the past eleven years will make things easier," Adam said.

"True. But even if we walked away paupers, I wouldn't give a fuck as long as they were in my life."

Adam laughed. "Are you getting sappy and sentimental in your old age?"

"You're the same age as me, asshole."

Adam chuckled. "I'll see you in a couple of weeks."

"Sounds good..."-

"Oh, Orion?"

"Yes?"

"Don't fuck this up." I could hear his smile on the other end.

"I did that once. Learned my lesson."

"Good."

Andee read the prenup about three times before she signed. She got everything. I didn't worry about her leaving me. Leaving us, so the fifty/fifty split bullshit wasn't necessary. It was more for show than for anything.

The engagement ring I gave her had a round diamond for Aries, a ruby for Leo, and a sapphire for me, all three entwined around a deep red garnet for Andromeda, our queen. Garnets represent fire within softness, light shifting beneath the surface, and unpredictable brilliance. All three qualities that represent Andee perfectly.

"We are all together, entwined with you, little flame, and you with us." She got on her tiptoes and kissed me, then Leo and Aries.

"Thank you," she murmured, admiring her ring.

"We need to figure out a date for the wedding," I said.

"Does it have to be soon?"

I raised a brow at her.

She huffed out a laugh, rolling her eyes at me. "That's not what I meant, you silly man. I meant, for planning purposes."

I smiled. "Ahh, well, that is no issue. I have the perfect wedding coordinator picked out."

She put her hands on her hips. "What? How could you just decide like..."-

Andee's cousin, Olivia, came through the door and onto the balcony.

"Olivia?"

"Hey little cousin," Olivia smiled as. the two embraced. Olivia's mother was Maeve's sister. She'd been overseas for the past eight years, working as a contractor for one of the ABC government agencies.

"I'm so sorry about your parents," Olivia said. "I'm so sorry I wasn't there."

Andee shook her head. "It's okay, Olivia, really. I wasn't alone."

Olivia smiled coyly, looking at the three of us. "I can see that."

Pink bloomed on Andee's cheeks. "Livi!"

"Anyway! Where is my newest cousin?"

"I'll take you to the nursery," Andee said, linking her arm with her cousin's, and the two walked off.

Aries raised a brow. "Olivia, huh?"

"What? She was a wedding coordinator."

"*Was* being the optimal word," he snickered.

Leo chuckled. "Doesn't have anything to do with the fact that she can kill a man ten different ways, does it?"

"I mean, it was a perk, no doubt." A smile arched my lips.

I trusted Andee to be safe with Olivia, and though I'd still worry, we all would; at least this way Andee could get somewhat of a normal wedding experience. Not that any of this was normal; far from it. This was our first united stance against the Romano's, and we knew they would hit back. The only question was when.

Andee

My cousin was actually here. I hadn't seen her in at least ten years. I was always the annoying little cousin, acting like Olivia's shadow. But she always made time for me, going on adventures together around the city.

She worked for her mom's wedding coordinating business, then went to work for a government agency. It was quite a career change. Her parents moved to Europe somewhere, and she decided she wanted to see the world too. So she signed up when she was twenty-one.

Olivia was holding Cassie, cooing over her when Daphne walked into the nursery.

"I heard you were here, Olivia! This is so exciting!"

"Nice to see you, Daphne," Olivia said with a smile. She turned back to Cassie, who grabbed her finger.

"She is the most precious thing, cousin. She looks like you when you were a baby," she said with a soft smile.

"Except for her eyes," I noted with a little smile.

"Definitely Orion's," she said with a laugh.

Daphne sat on the end of the bed in the guest room Orion had prepared for Olivia, and my cousin took in the opulence of the room.

"Andee was just about to spill the tea about her three men." Her laughter filled the room.

I swatted at her leg. "I was not!"

She scrunched her nose. "Come on, cuz, not even a little?"

"If you don't, I will," Daphne threatened with a teasing laugh.

I felt my cheeks warm.

I'd literally been fucked by my men on the dining room table, and yet I couldn't even say the words in front of my cousin and best friend.

"Such a little prude," Olivia teased.

"Oh! That is the last thing she is!" Daphne cackled.

"No fair, it's two against one!" I said with a laugh I couldn't keep in.

Between planning the wedding and spending most days and nights going through files, the next month flew by. We'd been working on allowing the mirror program to show enough 'progress' that it triggered protocols in the Romano's beta programs, without messing everything up and releasing the entire program.

I'd stared at the architecture of the program for days, scrolling through lines of predictive branches, knowing there was a rhythm beneath, but not being able to find it. The data wasn't random; it was pulsing, expanding and contracting, but every time I thought I'd found the sequence, it would slip sideways into something else entirely, as if the program was changing its makeup right in front of me. I was trying to work backward, trying to deconstruct my father's thought patterns, how he created the program. It might as well have been in Latin or something, because none of it made sense.

The looming stress of the Cosa Nostra and the wedding wasn't making anything easier, and to top it off, Cassie started teething, and we started her on baby cereal, so to say it was a lot would be the understatement of the century. I was very proud that I wasn't experiencing an existential crisis.

Then, before I knew it, it was the night of the rehearsal dinner, here at the villa, with mostly just close friends and a few associates of the guys. I was taken aback when Orion introduced me to Nikolai "Kolya" Sokolov. He went to university with Orion. I could tell he was a man of few words, but he was taking everything in.

I felt Aries' arms around my waist, and his lips brushed against my neck, and I leaned into his touch.

"If you think any harder, kitten, smoke will come out of your ears," he teased.

"Is the man Orion's talking to part of the Bratva?" I asked with concern lacing my tone.

"Kolya is the son of Nikolai, who served as an operations lieutenant under the Pakhan in St. Petersburg. He handled logistics, transport, and 'problem resolution.' The kind of man who handled the things that don't exist on paper. He's not officially Bratva, but exists on the outskirts. Consulting on security systems, digital infrastructure, and money movement. He understands both the technical and the physical leverage."

My shoulders relaxed a touch.

"He's here because we may need his connections," Aries explained.

I turned my head to face him. "He can be trusted?"

Aries smiled. "Yes, kitten, he can. He wouldn't be here if we didn't." Aries' hand grazed my ass. "You are *killing me* in this dress." His lips brushed against my ear and his hard cock was pressed against my ass. "How bad would it look if I fucked the bride-to-be at her engagement party? Bend her over and fuck her someplace someone might walk in."

My breath hitched at his words, and my panties were officially ruined.

"I think she'd like it," he chuckled darkly and guided me down the hall and into the library.

The smell of ink and old paper filled my nose as Aries' gaze burned into me, stalking me until I bumped into one of the chairs. He spun me around, smacking my ass, and a little squeak escaped me as he bent me over the arm of a chair, pulled my dress over my ass, kicking my legs apart as he shoved my panties aside. One hand found its way around my throat, his cock pressed against my entrance.

"Such a messy little cunt," Aries rasped in my ear as he fucked me, pressing his hand around my throat. "You'll do anything to be fucked, even risk being walked in on so they can see you bent over with my cock inside you."

His words made me shiver as he fucked me hard and deep. "Fuck Aries! God, yes! Please fuck me harder!"

He smacked my ass and my pussy fluttered; a guttural growl reverberated from his chest.

"Good girl, choke my cock with your little cunt."

I pressed his hand tighter against my throat.

"What's your safe word?" He rasped.

"Stars," I cried out as he put more pressure on my throat, the sensation making everything a million times more intense.

"Yes! I'm...I'm going to come! Fuccck!"

I exploded, my pussy clenching Aries' cock as he growled possessively and filled me with his cum. He fucked me through the waves of my orgasm.

I slumped against the chair. "Holy hell," I wheezed.

Aries pulled out and helped me clean up in the bathroom. I tried to make myself presentable as a coy smile passed Aries' lips.

"Just how I love seeing you, freshly fucked."

I felt my cheeks warm, and he kissed me, pulling me into his arms. The door opened and my heart fluttered.

Orion stepped into the room. His pupils dilating, and a low rumble left his chest.

"If you're quite finished fucking my fiancee, there are some people who would like to meet her." The two shared a look that would make some people think Orion was pissed off. But he wasn't, and I didn't need his eyes to tell me that; his cock straining against his pants told me all I needed to know. He pulled me into his arms.

"Next time, I want to watch your little cunt get filled, understand, little flame?"

"Yes, Daddy."

"Good girl." His deep, raspy voice had my knees nearly buckling.

"Orion, I swear if you try coming in here," Daphne warned, her brows knitted at not just Orion, but Leo and Aries as well. "You will survive one night without her!"

She pushed the door closed, literally in their faces, turned and leaned against the door as I chuckled.

"They are insatiable! My god! It's one fucking night!" She let out a loud huff, rolling her eyes.

Daphne and Olivia insisted that the men not see me before the wedding, so at eleven fifty-five, they 'stole' me and whisked me into Daphne's room. We were having a very tiny bachelorette party. Olivia and Daphne had drinks, and I was having sparkling grape juice. I sat back on the bed, leaning my head against the soft headboard.

"You good?" Daphne asked, pouring herself another drink from the bar.

"Yes," I sighed.

"I cannot wait for their jaws to drop when they see you tomorrow," Daphne said with a little laugh.

I laughed at my friend, "Me either." A smile crossed my lips as I looked at my ring from Orion, well from all of them, really. The intertwined gems representing our birth months made my heart happy whenever I looked at it.

"I'm excited, but there's a part of me that is a little sad," I admitted.

Olivia smiled. "I can imagine. I mean, you're in a pretty unique situation; it's not like everyone is banging three sexy as fuck, powerful men." Her laughter filled the space as I threw a pillow at her.

"Goofball! I meant that as much as I know it's just a piece of paper, there's a bigger meaning to it. I want to say the vows to all of them, not just Orion."

Daphne shrugged. "So have another ceremony, just the four of you. It won't be legal, but who the fuck cares?"

"I like that idea," I said, with a smile forming. I felt a little lighter about everything.

I was dreaming and suddenly; I felt something touch my leg, then a hand over my mouth. Panic filled me as my eyes popped open and my fight-or-flight response kicked in.

"Shhh, little flame," Orion's deep eyes met mine, as his hand wrapped around my throat and he smiled deviously. He didn't say anything else; he simply lifted me out of the bed, my legs wrapped around his waist, and he took me outside, my back hitting the wall as his mouth captured mine.

He shoved my panties aside with one hand and then undid his pants, his cock pressing against my entrance, and I moaned his name while he nipped at my neck with a possessive growl.

"You're wet, my little toy, aren't you? My hand around your throat when I woke you excited you, didn't it?"

I moaned as he thrust inside my pussy. He smacked my ass, and I moaned even louder.

"I asked you a question," he rumbled.

"Yes, Daddy," I cried out as his cock hit the spot over and over as his hand wrapped around my throat.

"What's your safe word?" He growled.

"Stars," I hissed as he fucked me harder; his intense, possessive look made my pussy clench.

"Good little toy, milk my cock, I'm going to fill you with my cum."

"Fuck, yes, Daddy, please, fuck me harder."

His lips nipped against my throat as he continued to fuck me hard and deep. The pressure on my throat tightened. "I want you to come on my cock, now!"

A scream ripped from my throat as my entire body shuddered, and I felt his release. He fucked me until I stopped shaking; kissed me possessively, and then set me down, holding onto me as I tried to stand on my own.

He chuckled darkly. "I take what's mine whenever I want, little flame, remember that," he rasped against my ear as he guided me back into the room, then the bathroom to clean me up.

He pushed the covers aside; I slid into bed, and he kissed me, then disappeared back into the shadows.

Orion

The observation tower is my favorite structure on the island. It rises above the cliff-side like something ancient and deliberate. A circular structure of pale stone and glass built right into the rock face. During the day it looks architectural, impressive but grounded. But at night, it becomes something else entirely. I left the wedding plans to Olivia and Andee, except for the venue. That was my only request. Because marrying Andee anywhere else wouldn't have been worthy of her.

The dome above us was glass, curving overhead without interruption, and when the lights were dimmed, the sky swallowed us whole. The Mediterranean stretched into the darkness below, invisible except for the faint silver shimmer of the moonlight on the water, but up here, up here there was nothing but stars. No city glare. No sound but distant waves against stone. Up here, wrapped in night and silence and constellations, it felt as if the rest of the world couldn't touch us.

I stood with Leo on my right and Aries on my left. The entire room was lined with fancy tables on either side, decorated in shades of blue with touches of silver. The guest list, which included government officials, business associates, and friends, disappeared. It was only her I saw; the only sound I heard was my racing heart.

She didn't choose white. Of course she didn't.

Nothing about Andee had ever been conventional, and I should have known she wouldn't start now. The moment she stepped beneath the domed glass, the shades of blue in her dress caught every flicker of candlelight and every distant star above us. She was never meant for something traditional.

She was meant to command the sky.

The gown shimmered like a living constellation, clinging to her curves before spilling into something soft and endless, like the universe itself had knelt at her feet. Her hair fell in golden waves down her back, and when she lifted her chin, the blue depths of her eyes made her look less like a bride and more like something celestial. She is as unique as the stars overhead: countless, brilliant, impossible to replicate, and standing there, watching her walk toward me wrapped in the night itself, I realized something dangerous.

I don't just love her.

I worship her.

The ceremony was a blur; the noise of guests congratulating us, the toasts, and the music were just background noise. I couldn't wait to get her out of her dress and worship her properly, like the goddess she was.

I whisked her away, probably earlier than society would dictate, but society could kiss my ass. I opened the bridal suite, and I pushed her against the door, a growl rumbling from my chest as she melted against me.

"You are the most beautiful woman in the world, and while this dress is stunning, it still pales compared to you, my little wife."

Her breath hitched, and she moaned against my mouth.

She pushed me away, and I landed in one of the chairs as she sauntered toward me, slowly unzipping her dress. It pooled at her feet, and she was wearing all pink lingerie, with a garter belt and stockings. She straddled my lap and her hands ran through my hair as I possessively nipped down her neck, unhooking her bra, and I nipped and sucked her perfect breasts. Her head fell back, pressing her rosy nipples even closer, and I sucked so hard her thighs clenched.

"Oh my God," she murmured against my neck.

I nipped and sucked, barely touching the other nipple with my fingertips. I didn't let go as her hands grasped my shoulders and her thighs clenched again.

"Fuccckk, Orion, please don't stop."

Spurred on by her pussy rubbing against my aching cock, I continued until she cried out my name, her thighs shaking, and her pussy fluttering. I let her go with a wet pop, and her head fell onto my shoulder.

"Did you come, my little flame?" I asked with a dark chuckle.

"Holy mother of God. Yes." She barely got the words out.

"As much as I want to fuck you right now, I want to worship you even more, so let's get you into something else and we can go home."

"Yes, please," she mewled against my neck.

Once she was in another dress, I opened the door, and sitting on a wooden table in the hall was an enormous vase of white roses with a card sticking out of the top.

"Orion, did you?" She smiled.

"I wish I could take credit, but sadly, I cannot."

"It's okay," she said with a soft laugh. "They die way too fast, anyway." She pulled the card out.

"Congratulations on the wedding. Innocent as it may appear, some images have a way of rewriting stories."

Another paper fell out of the envelope; she unfolded it and let out an audible gasp.

Her eyes snapped to mine, narrowing. "Orion? What the hell is this?" Her cry of anger made my heart squeeze. I took the photo from her. This wasn't the one from the gala. This was from her twenty-first birthday.

"Did you know about this?" Her tone was cold and distant.

Leo and Aries walked over just as I was about to answer.

"Did you two know about this?" She hissed at them. They stopped dead in their tracks, both of them looking between the photo and me.

Aries put his hands up in surrender. "kitten, listen.."-

Her eyes narrowed. "Don't you dare 'kitten' me right now," she hissed. Her gaze snapped back to me. "Did.Yo u.Know?"

I slowly nodded.

"And why am I just finding out about this now? What the ever living fuck? What does this mean? Are they going to put this out in public?"

"We don't know," I admitted slowly.

Leo shook his head. "This was meant to do exactly this, baby girl. Divide us."

Aries' and Leo's eyes met mine. Andee noticed.

"What?" She asked.

Aries rubbed the back of his neck. "It's just.." -

"It's just what Aries?"

"That's not the first one."

Andee's fists clenched, scrunching the paper. "What do you mean? What was the other one?"

"The summer gala when you were eighteen," I admitted.

She let out an actual growl and walked away. Leo reached out for her wrist, but she yanked it away.

"Don't." She bit out at him as she stormed off, muttering curses as she went.

Aries winced. "That went well."

"We can't keep shit from her," Leo whispered.

"I know," I said, shaking my head as I slumped against the wall.

Andee

The photo of me and the guys at my twenty-first birthday made my blood run cold. It was a shit ending to a perfect day. I was livid. I asked Olivia bring me back to the villa. She didn't say anything until we pulled into the long driveway. Then she reached for my hand.

"I'm sure they meant well, Andee," she said.

"Maybe. But that doesn't excuse it. We're in this together."

"They've always been protective of you. And they've loved you for a long time."

My eyes met hers. I knew they loved me by their actions, looks, kisses, and how we connected when we were together. I was still mad at them; I needed to cool off.

I went into Cassie's room and told Elena she could have the rest of the night off. Cassie was babbling and cooing in her crib. I was feeding her when Orion came into the room.

I kept my eyes on Cassie; she held onto my hand as I fed her.

"Listen," Orion said, as he ran his hand through his hair.

"Don't. I don't want excuses." My eyes met his. "I want you to promise never to do something like that again. No matter how much you think it's for the best or will upset me."

"It won't happen again, I promise."

"Good."

"Where's Elena?"

"In her room. I gave her the rest of the night off."

"Oh," I heard the disappointment in his tone.

"Promise or not, Orion. I need some time."

"I get that," he said. "I'm sorry, little flame."

I didn't look up at him or respond, so he closed the partition.

The following morning, I slipped out of Daphne's room and found Orion reading on the terrace. His eyes met mine as I reached for the coffee.

"Morning," he said softly.

"Morning," I answered, then took a sip.

He reached his hand out, and his eyes were full of regret. He didn't have to say the words; his eyes told me everything he was feeling. I walked to his chair, and he pulled me onto his lap.

"I'm sorry, little flame," he murmured.

"We're in this together, and I don't want to be left out, Orion."

He closed his eyes and nodded, placing his forehead against mine.

"It won't happen again. I promise."

"Thank you," I answered, and he kissed me softly.

He scooped me up and brought me into the suite, locking the door. I raised a brow at him. "Call me a selfish bastard, I don't care. All I care about is that perfect pussy wrapped around my cock."

Holy mother of God.

After taking a few days to recoup from the wedding, I was focused on ending everything with the Atlas program. I knew the guys would keep us safe, but that didn't mean I would sit on the sidelines. I sat at one of the computer stations; things weren't going well, and it left me growling at the computer.

"Have you tried unplugging and plugging it back in?" Aries said with a chuckle as he walked in.

"Ha ha," I said with an eye roll.

Later, I was halfway through isolating a block of code, something buried deep, repeating in patterns that didn't quite match the rest.

"The further I go into this, the less sense it makes," I huffed.

"Um, baby girl, what did you just do?" Leo asked, his brows knitted.

"What do you mean?"

He pointed to his computer, "The code is breaking apart," he said with concern lacing his tone.

I jumped up from my seat and rushed over to him. "I don't know. Fuck!" I raced back to my computer, trying to reverse whatever I had just done, except I didn't know what I had done.

"I..I can't stop it!" An icy chill washed over me. I was clammy and my heartbeat rose.

"It was a code in both systems," Aries said, typing away. "It matches the mirror system, and now..."

"It tripped something in their system, fuck!"

I was so mad at myself.

It didn't look any different from the rest, just another line buried in thousands, but the more I pulled at it, the more the systems started crossing in ways they weren't supposed to. And then something on their end stalled... like I'd tripped a wire I didn't know was there.

A hush fell over the room, and I laid my head in my hands, shaking my head. "I can't believe I did that," I murmured.

I felt a hand reaching for mine. "How were you supposed to know, baby girl?" Leo asked, wrapping his arms around me.

I melted into him. "I...fuck. I don't know."

"Exactly," Aries said, rubbing my back. "This is all new to all of us. We're working in the dark here."

"But what if I just royally screwed something up?"

"Then we figure it out." Orion's voice wrapped around me.

Orion's phone rang, and the hair pricked up on my neck. "Hello?"

"Hello, Mr. Kane, my name is Robert Lampert from The Financial Vanguard. I was wondering if I could ask you a few questions regarding the timing of your marriage to Andromeda Voss?"

His jaw clenched. "Absolutely not. No comment."

"I understand, Mr. Kane, but I just want to let you know we have information here that will provide us enough to publish an expose. The information we received makes the timing extremely questionable."

"And your source?"

"That is confidential, sir."

"You will be hearing from my attorney. Good day."

He ended the call.

"Those fuckers!" he roared, slamming the phone down. His jaw clenched so hard, I was shocked he didn't break a tooth. He started to turn and walk out. "I need to make a couple of calls."

"Calls to whom?" I asked. I was worried. I did fuck something up.

"First to Adam. I need to get ahead of this."

"Then who?" I asked.

"A journalist I know. If they want to play this game of making the other look bad in the press, I can play even harder."

I bit my lip as Orion walked to where I was and wrapped his arms around me. "This is how they work, little flame. We aren't just working within our own world right now. We're playing in their playground, and they are going to use tactics that will try to get us to make mistakes."

"I understand," I said. "Just how bad is this for us?"

"I won't lie to you. It's not good. But that's what I pay Adam for," he said with a small smile, trying to ease her mind at least a little.

"He can get them to stop?"

He kissed me. "I am certain of it."

Later in the day, I was sitting by the pool deck. The entire area was surrounded by trees, which allowed us to enjoy the beautiful view of the sea, but it was secluded. The infinity pool sat next to a hot tub; huge padded loungers and blue umbrellas covered the area while letting enough sun in to warm my skin as I sat reading. I read and re-read the same line about a dozen times. I couldn't concentrate. I was trying to figure out where I went wrong, how I didn't see that the lines of code weren't connected. None of it made sense, and I was frustrated as fuck.

A shadow covered my body. I looked up to see Orion, in swim trunks, his chiseled, tanned chest glistening, leading down to his delicious V. I swallowed hard as his gaze stopped at my cleavage. My swimsuit was navy with silver, and the V between my breasts stopped nearly at my belly button. He moved around to my side, sliding behind me. I was so entranced by him, it was too late to realize the cover of my book was showing.

"What are you reading?" I didn't need to look at him to know he was smiling.

I felt my cheeks get warm. "Nothing," I said, closing the book.

"The cover tells me otherwise, little flame."

"It's a fantasy romance, okay?" I said with a touch of embarrassment. Though why I was embarrassed, I had no idea. I'd been reading spicy novels for years.

"What's it about?"

"Greek demigods, the sons of Zeus, Hades, and Poseidon, and the daughter of Athena," I answered, biting my bottom lip.

He slid the book out of my hand and set it on the chair next to ours. He pulled me closer, his lips ghosting near my ear. "The things I plan on doing to you would make the characters in your smutty romance book blush."

My heartbeat rose and my breath caught as he kissed me down my neck, his hand inching toward my thighs.

"Spread those legs for me like a good girl," he rasped against my neck as his teeth trailed down, making a hiss escape me.

My thighs parted at his command, and his fingers teased my pussy, barely touching my clit with the tip of his finger as his other hand ghosted one of my nipples, sending shockwaves through my body as my head fell back onto his chest.

"I barely have to touch you and you're already wet for me, aren't you, little flame?"

"Yes, Daddy," I moaned as he continued barely touching my most sensitive areas, yet the sensation was making me arch and buck for more friction.

One finger became two as he pumped in and out of my pussy.

"So tight, so perfect," he rasped against me as he slid one strap of my bathing suit down, then the other, so I was bared for him. He flipped me around so I was straddling him as he sucked on my nipple, making my pussy flutter against his hard cock.

"See what you do to me, little flame?" He rasped as he pushed his hips up so my pussy was grinding against his cock.

"Please, Daddy," I moaned as my hips moved. "I need you inside me, please."

"Take out my cock," he rasped. I freed his enormous cock, and I slid down, seating myself until he was fully inside me. He let out a hiss, and his eyes turned possessive.

"Now, ride my cock like a good girl."

I circled my hips, slightly raising and lowering myself on him. His tongue flicked my nipple as he tugged on the other. I sucked in a breath, the pleasure and pain sensation had my pussy clenching as I fucked myself on his cock. He leaned his head back against the chair, and his eyes closed.

"Fuck, yesss," he hissed. Just like that."

I clenched around him again, loving the fact that I was making him lose himself. His head shot up and his eyes darkened as I continued to clench and unclench around his cock. A little squeak escaped my lips as he flipped me onto my knees, and he plunged himself inside me. His hands dug into my hips as he fucked me hard and deep.

"What's your safe word?" He hissed out as he fucked me harder.

"Starrsss!" I screamed as he hit the spot over and over. His hand reached around my throat and the pressure made my pussy flutter and clench around him. His low growl sent shivers down my spine.

"I want you to come, little flame."

My body obeyed as my orgasm hit, and I shattered around him, screaming his name as I felt him come inside me.

Our breaths were ragged, and he kissed my neck. He lifted me and my legs wrapped around him as we walked us to a small little building I hadn't noticed before.

"You have a shower out here?" I said with a chuckle.

"Chlorine is terrible for your skin, and even though the pool is mostly saltwater, it's best to get it off as soon as possible."

I chuckled. "I've been here for months, and I am still discovering places I've never seen."

His eyes sparkled, and a smile arched his lips. "In," he said with a little pinch on my ass. A squeak escaped me as I got into the shower; he followed.

We cleaned up, and he put me into a fluffy robe, and he did the same. We sat together and had lunch brought to us on the pool deck, along with a fruity frozen virgin drink for me and a whisky for him. Sitting together, me wrapped in his arms; the conversation flowed naturally, and we talked about everything and nothing, and I loved every second and I wished it didn't have to end. But I reminded myself: the sooner we got this all over with, the sooner we could have more days like this.

Leo

The back and forth between us and Romano really took shape when Adam threatened the reporter; and the story vanished. Then Orion's journalist contact released a story about the illegitimacy of a child of Dante Romano. They retaliated with a compliance inquiry into one of Centari's subsidiaries, triggered by an anonymous filing that questioned the legitimacy of one of our newest security frameworks from an unknown advisory firm. We squeezed one of the companies they had acquired, sending a virus through their system which made every shipping manifest be questioned because of weight discrepancies. Then, a charity board Orion was on suddenly requested documentation for donations that had been cleared years earlier. It was a back-and-forth game of chicken.

Each move was small on its own, but it kept us busy. I dismantled the regulatory inquiry in twenty-four hours. Orion leaned on a few key charity board members until their hesitation vanished. I traced an advisory firm back to a Romano holding company, stopping three more 'regulatory' inquiries and audits that they were planning. The Romanos tried very hard to stay invisible. None of it damaged us. But that wasn't the point. The Romanos were showing us exactly how easily they could reach into our world.

The back and forth was getting exhausting, so the five of us sat down with a risk assessment Aries had compiled based on things that the Romano's had access to not only through the program,

"This could last for years and could escalate," Aries said with a frustrated sigh. "So we either continue this and risk them upping the ante, or we pull the trigger. This is not sustainable."

Orion shook his head. "I agree, it's time to cross over into the real world. Physical pressure points that will make the Romanos lose focus on us."

"So we're agreed then?" Aries asked, looking at Andee, then at me.

She blew out a breath. "Yes."

"Yes," I answered.

Orion called Kolai, and he set us up to meet in an area of London that we'd not stepped foot in for a long time. The West End of London is where all the people wanted to be seen. Velvet ropes, long lines of patrons, and the thump of music surrounded us as we stepped into Obsidian, a club owned by Dimitri Volkov, Pakhan of the Bratva in London. We stepped into the club; the dance floor was full of bodies moving to the beat of the pulsing music. Black marble tables with black velvet bucket seats lined either side of the dance floor as we were led up a staircase to the VIP section.

"The Pakhan will be here shortly," a tall man said. "In the meantime, would anyone care for a drink?"

We all declined as we sat in black bucket chairs, Andee next to Orion. She was both excited and nervous to come with us. Leaving Cassie at the villa for the first time since the interaction with Matteo was making her anxious, but Olivia had been staying with us since the wedding, deciding on a job offer, so between her and Daphne, they were texting Andee at least every hour with updates.

The Pakhan strolled into the VIP section in his all black designer suit, black shirt and black silk tie, unbuttoning his jacket as he sat like a king in his audience chamber. Nikolai made the introductions, and we got down to business. We started by showing him the security network we could provide him. When he found out we had breached his system, his eyes narrowed for a split second, and his hand clasped his glass harder, but there was no other change in his look or demeanor.

"Not that I do not believe what you say, Mr. Kane, but I would like to have my men see for themselves."

"No offense taken," Orion said as one of his men made a call, then handed the phone to the Pakhan. He spoke to whomever on the other end in Russian, then ended the call.

"My team should get back to me shortly. In the meantime, tell me more of your proposal."

"The Cosa Nostra is attempting to monopolize predictive intelligence that would destabilize commodity markets and sovereign risk forecasting. Controlled volatility benefits energy corridors, but algorithmic dominance threatens them. If the Cosa Nostra gains full predictive leverage, no underground economy remains insulated. What we are offering, in return for controlled strikes that feel coincidental, is access to a defensive portion of one of our proprietary systems," I explained. "It would be for counter surveillance, data shielding, and threat detection."

The Pakhan leaned back slightly, his sharp gaze moving between the three of us. "This is a risk for us, and not so much for you."

Orion didn't hesitate. "Centari secures infrastructure," he said evenly. "Digital and physical. Financial routing, communication networks, logistics channels; anything that needs to exist without interference. You become invisible."

A faint, but skeptical smile touched the Pakhan's mouth. "Invisible is a word many men use when they are trying to sell me something."

I leaned forward a touch. "Not invisible in theory," I said calmly. "Invisible in architecture. Layered encryption, isolated routing nodes, mirrored authentication chains. If someone breaches the outer network, they will never see what matters."

"Right now, your system relies on concealment," Aries added. "Centari builds systems that survive exposure."

He considered us and our offer. Then a man whispered in his ear. Again, the Pakhan showed no change in emotion.

"You say my system was easily manipulated. Show me how you would fix it." He snapped his fingers, and a man appeared with a laptop. Walking toward Orion, he then turned and handed it to Andee instead.

She didn't say a word; she simply opened the laptop, her hands furiously clicking on the keys; The Pakhan watched her with interest, and we watched with bated breath. We knew she could do anything he asked, but no matter what I thought Andee was capable of, she always surprised me.

A map of financial routing nodes and logistics channels popped up on the screen. Ports, holding companies, transport hubs, threats of movement running through Europe like veins. A small section near London pulsed red, then shifted to green.

"You run three layers of shell routing through this logistics chain," Andee explained. "It's clever, but the second layer leaks metadata every six minutes through customs monitoring back channels. She tapped the screen, turning it for the Pakhan to see. "The Romanos are already testing it."

Andee closed the computer and leaned back slightly, her voice steady. "I patched it while I was in the system. Consider it a show of goodwill."

The room went still.

"You asked what Centari could do for you," she added. "That was a fragment of just one system we have. Imagine what could happen if you had access to the entire system."

The Pakhan considered her for several long seconds. I was holding in a breath as he measured her face, studying her. Then he smiled faintly.

"Let's discuss a timeframe for setting up Centari based on the targets we meet. We will exchange them for access to your system."

He reached across the table, his hand extended toward Andee. She extended her hand, and the two sealed the deal.

The attack on the Cosa Nostra was like a well-choreographed dance, and the Bratva's attacks all lined up better than we had expected. Things were finally moving in a way that made us all feel a little more confident. The Bratva struck in ways that felt coincidental. The first was a gold shipment tied to a Cosa Nostra front company that was delayed at port because of sudden regulatory scrutiny. A private equity collapsed when financing was quietly withdrawn and re-invested in one of the Bratva's holding companies. Key logistic corridors experienced 'unexpected' inspections that froze supply chains for days.

The final nail in the coffin was the Bratva increasing the pressure on institutions whose leaders frequented their clubs and other underground entertainment venues. Secrets were currency, and since the Bratva owned a lot of these types of businesses, the Romano's would not be the only ones to feel regulatory pressure. The plan was to go after other families in the Cosa Nostra as well. But that was waiting until we were finished with Atlas Sentinel completely. So the 'attacks' on the Romano's were slowed, but they were so busy defending themselves to the other families and 'cleaning house,' they basically forgot about us.

Andee had still been doing her best to reverse engineer the Atlas program. The concern about the Romanos using it to attack us wasn't as much of a concern, but Andee wanted to stop the program. It was too much of a risk to keep it.

Andee turned her chair around and cleared her throat. "Okay, so I've run a hundred models," Andee said confidently. "Each time it failed, I tried a different set of parameters and numbers."

Aries raised a brow, a small smile arching his lips. "And just how many successful runs did you have?"

She gave him a coy smile back. "One."

Orion tried not to smile. "Maybe we should run it a few more times, just in case?"

She rolled her eyes. "Fine." She spun her chair around and got to work. I didn't miss the tilt of her lips, though, and it made me smile.

Andee was asleep at her desk. The screen's blue glow was the only light in the room. I didn't want to disturb her, but it was late and she'd been sitting at the computer for days, almost non-stop. Aries and Orion had both found her in the middle of the night a few days ago, and we insisted on a screen-free weekend. Something we all needed.

But she was determined to figure it out. She knew Atlas didn't start out for the program to end up like it did, and I could tell she was sad destroying her dad's work, but we all knew it was the best.

I walked to where she was and I scooped her up in my arms. The little mewl sound that escaped her lips made my cock twitch.

"Leo?" She asked sleepily.

"Shh, let's get you to bed."

"But I wasn't finished," she mumbled. Barely able to lift her arm to point toward her computer station.

"You've run models all day and night, baby girl. You need your rest." I kissed her on the temple as I carried her into our suite. Aries and Orion were meeting with various entities in London, and I was being a selfish bastard staying back with Andee. I had two whole nights of her all to myself.

Her breasts spilled free from her shirt as I lifted it over her head and her nipples peaked. She wiggled out of her shorts and then lay on the bed. I lay next to her; she wiggled her perfect little ass into my cock. I ran my hand down her neck and she sleepily mumbled my name like a prayer.

"Leo, please," she murmured.

"Please, what, baby girl?" I mouthed against her neck.

"Please fuck me."

I turned her toward me and raised her leg over my thigh. I kissed her neck, lowering to her breasts, sucking on each nipple as she arched into me. My fingers found her folds, and I rumbled against her neck.

"I haven't even touched you and you're already wet for me, aren't you, baby?"

"Mhmm," She murmured, touching the tip of my cock, making me hiss.

I pressed my cock into her tight heat and moved my hips. I ran my hand down her back, near her ass, caressing her, which drove her crazy. Her body arched against mine as I moved my hand closer to her ass, and she moaned as my hips moved faster, and her little pussy clenched around my cock.

I nipped at her ear. "Such a good girl clenching my cock with your tight little pussy."

We found our rhythm together as I circled her clit with my fingers. I pinched her clit and sucked on her nipple, and her body shuddered.

"Fuck, yes, please don't stop, Leo. Fuck...I'm going to...-Fuckkk!"

"Milk my cock with your tight little cunt," I rumbled as she choked my cock, spurring my own release.

"Fuck," I rumbled against her neck, then captured her lips with mine.

I lifted her into the bathroom, cleaned both of us up, then brought her back to the bed. I covered us and pulled her against me. I was hard again in a matter of seconds, but she let out a soft yawn, and as much as I'd like to have fucked her the rest of the night, I kissed her neck, "Go to sleep, baby girl."

It was the best kind of torture. And I was more than willing to endure it for the rest of my life if it meant her in my arms every night.

Aries

Orion and I were dropped off at the front of the villa, and Andee was practically bouncing on her toes as Orion and I walked through the door.

Andee had Cassie in a front carrier, and she was babbling away. Orion's eyes met Andee's, and he kissed her, then he gave Cassie a kiss on her head and I tried to wait patiently, but he hovered, so I teasingly pushed him out of the way, capturing Andee's mouth as she let out a small laugh that made my heart melt.

"How were the meetings?" She asked.

Orion rolled his eyes. "Boring as ever."

Andee bit her bottom lip. "I think it's ready," she said with a little nervous chuckle.

Orion raised a brow.

Leo smiled. "She's run fifty more models just today; they all acting the same."

"That sounds promising," Orion said as we walked toward the computer room.

"And I put a wall between Atlas and our systems, nothing will affect our operations," I told them.

"Well, you two were certainly busy," Aries teased with his double meaning comment. Andee's cheeks bloomed pink, and Aries chuckled.

Andee walked Cassie to her room and re-joined us as we stepped into the computer room. The screen was prepped for Andee to execute the command. Her hand hovered over the button. She blew out a breath as the three of us sat at our stations to monitor our current systems and the markets. Andee gave Leo a nod. He would shut down the air-gap system for good. The beta program would collapse on its own once the Atlas program ended.

"Here goes nothing." She pressed the button.

The system executed the command, and it folded inward exactly as the projections and tests predicted. Then it stopped.

Screens exploded with motion. Data multiplied across the interface, branching new predictive paths faster than the processors should have been able to generate them. Routing nodes that should have shut down...simply didn't. The architecture reassembled itself in real time, redirecting streams, absorbing external signals, building new frameworks to replace ones that had just been destroyed.

Andee's breath caught. "That..that's not possible, she murmured. The look in her eyes told me the models didn't fail. She caught her mistake, and her face fell. "All of my simulations have been mathematic...fuck."

The program wasn't reacting like a machine. Across the monitors, the escalation module responded to the shutdown attempt with controlled countermeasures; it was adapting and measuring, almost tactical. She looked like she had been punched in the gut.

"I wasn't thinking like my dad. I was thinking strategically, logically, predictively, anything to make it viable without causing a global meltdown."

All the color drained out of her face as the realization hit.

The system wasn't solving equations.

It was following instincts.

"You're thinking like us, little flame," Orion admitted.

Her gaze snapped to Orion, and like a lightbulb going off, she turned to her workstation.

"I need you all to tap into the system!" she said excitedly. She looked at the three of us, standing and looking back at her. "Now." She said with a little wave of her hand.

I felt a smile tug at the corners of my mouth as the three of us sat at our workstations.

"I was watching it wrong. Watching numbers instead of patterns." She explained as her fingers tapped furiously on the keyboard. "Dad didn't build just a program; he built a system that thought the way you all did. It's trying to survive because it thinks it's under attack. Not one of us can kill it alone," she said. "It will take *all* of us. Because he built all of you into it. The program thinks one of you is being attacked. He built things into it you all built for Centari. The protocols look different, and they are expanded, but it's all of you."

"See this one," she said, pointing to one of the layers that was shifting. "It's rerouting probabilities through branching contingencies that look exactly like the operational forecasts that you built, Orion, when planning security deployments. If we all go after our own 'layer', it won't think it's attacking just one of the systems."

"It won't know what to do," I said.

"Yes."

When we began the process, the system reacted immediately. As Leo cut the global financial feeds, economic data that gave it broad predictive power. In response, the program tried to compensate by expanding its threat-analysis modules, pulling in geopolitical signals and enforcement timing data. Then I stepped in, dismantling the escalation algorithms that allowed the system to scale conflict models. Without that layer, the program attempted to reroute its predictive lattice, searching for new pathways to rebuild its strategic awareness. Orion was up next, intercepting that adaptation, rewriting the strategic core so the system forecasts were confined to localized security parameters rather than global patterns. The architecture resisted every step, trying to correct itself, because survival was built into its logic.

Andee didn't activate a failsafe; there wasn't one. She wrote one in real time, embedding an ethical ceiling deep into the architecture while the system actively resisted her.

Then, for the first time, all the monitors stopped.

Andee had unshed tears in her eyes. "He built it so that the people he trusted most worked together. Each of you was part of the system, and together you make things balanced. Still formidable, keeping things in check."

"The world can overwhelm any of you. It will never overwhelm all of you." She murmured Atlas' words.

Orion touched her cheek, coxing her into his lap.

"I know he didn't intend for this to happen, but...*fuck.*"

Our phones started blowing up with text alerts, and news feeds scrolling across our phones.

"What did you do, kitten?" I asked with a smile arching his lips.

Andee shrugged her shoulders, a coy smile tugged at the corners of her lips. Orion's eyes sparkled. "Little flame?"

"The system logged every external probe the Romano's made while trying to understand Atlas. Instead of deleting records, I structured the logs into a forensic trail showing repeated attempts to mirror and extract pieces of Centari's proprietary code. Because technically the code belonged to Centari. They'll be drowning in probes, inquiries, espionage investigations and regulatory scrutiny for decades."

"When did you have time.." - I said, then stopped myself. I chuckled. "On second thought, I don't want to know."

She just gave me a little wink. The little firecracker.

Orion

A month after we shut down Atlas, we had to deal with regulatory board meetings and government contract re-negotiations, along with cleaning up the mess the Romanos made with all the security companies they had acquired. There are several firms that aren't as large as Centari, but still formidable, and we would sever those firms. As much as I wanted to keep them, it was better from a business standpoint.

I contacted Knox Helion, who owned Aegis Security, which specialized in private security for elite clientele. He was going to take over the private security firms that were like his. It would not be easy by any means, but if anyone could handle it, Knox could. He owned one of the largest casinos in Las Vegas. His two brothers provided the security for the talent, and they combined the businesses.

Five Months later

I don't know why I was nervous; the ceremony we planned was just us, Daphne, Olivia, and a few friends, but I felt more of a weight than I did when Andee and I got married the first time. Once things settled after the Romano nonsense. She approached me about having a ceremony for the four of us. She knew it wouldn't be legal, but she wanted the same connection with Aries and Leo as she had with me.

I, of course, was more than happy about it, and the guys were over the moon when she mentioned it. Little did we know she was pregnant. There wasn't a lot to plan, and we insisted it could wait, but she was more insistent, and of course, we didn't say no.

The three of us stood near the balcony of the villa as Andee approached, her belly round with our child. Any time I looked at her, my possessive nature took over, and even though we didn't know who the father was, it didn't matter; both Cassie and now this new baby would be all of ours.

She was stunning, and her petal pink dress accentuated the perfect swell of her breasts, and her hair looked like spun gold in the sunshine. She stood between us, and each of us stood breathless for a minute until Daphne cleared her throat with a teasing laugh. We did the traditional vows with Adam officiating. It was easier to have him become 'ordained' via the internet, instead of explaining to an actual priest that Andee was marrying three men.

Once the ceremony was over, we whisked our little wife off into our suite and didn't emerge for almost forty-eight hours. It was absolute bliss.

Before Andee, our business was our lives. With her in our lives, we understand that before her; we were simply surviving, and now we're living, and we aren't looking back.

Andee

One year later

Alexander toddled over to Leo, who scooped him up, and he giggled as Leo blew raspberries on his tummy. Cassie was sitting with Aries, who was reading her favorite book for the thirtieth time. I was sitting against Orion, watching Leo and Aries with our kids. That's how it had been since Cassie was born. DNA didn't matter to the men, nor to me.

Things had quieted down slowly; the men returned to their normal work schedules, and I took over some of the cyber-security side of Centari, which kept me busy. We were enjoying our time at the villa, having made it our permanent residence when I got pregnant with Alexander. Routines normalized as best they could while having two little ones, but there was still the occasional trip the men had to take for the company.

Orion brushed his lips against my neck, and goosebumps skated over my skin. His dark chuckle washed over me, and I could feel his lips tip into a smile.

"No fair," I murmured as both Leo and Aries looked at me at the same time.

"Remember what I told you, little flame, I take what's mine whenever I want. We warned you that a punishment for your little performance video text message was going to happen. You made all of us sit through our meeting with our cocks straining against our slacks."

I shivered at his words, and he scooped me up, throwing me over his shoulder. I watched Aries and Leo take the kids to Elena in the nursery and then follow us into our bedroom.

I watched three sets of eyes on me. Possessive and full of promise. I undressed, and three audible groans filled the air. They were mine, and I was theirs. Once I believed being with them was forbidden, but what we share is more rare than all the stars in the sky, something written long before us. And now that I've found it, I'm never letting it go.

The end.

If you loved Andee and her men's story, I hope you will consider leaving a review. I love sharing my stories, and reviews help others find my books. Thank you.
Gwendolyn

Coming Soon

Book 1 in the Astral
Veil Academy Series

When I received my acceptance to Astral Veil Academy, it should have felt like the beginning of everything I'd ever wanted. The most powerful students in the world train behind its walls—heirs of the Zodiac Houses destined to command the elements, protect the Harmony Barrier, and someday lead the Astral world itself. But unlike most at the academy, I can't access my magic. In a place where power determines your worth, being unmanifested isn't just humiliating...it's dangerous. If my abilities don't awaken soon, I'll lose my place at Astral Veil before I ever discover why I was brought there.

Then things start happening.

The professors insist no student has remained unmanifested for generations, claiming what's happening to me is simply a delayed awakening. But magic rarely makes the air stop moving when someone enters a room. It doesn't make storms spiral inside classrooms or silver mist form where there should only be wind. And it definitely doesn't make the Harmony Barrier pulse like something on the other side suddenly knows my name. The more they try to explain it away, the more terrified I become that this isn't an awakening at all—that something else is happening to me.

And I am starting to believe it's because of them.

Jace burns through every room he enters, reckless and devastating in ways that make it impossible to stay away from him. Theo hides razor-sharp control beneath calm smiles and blue eyes that seem to notice everything I try to hide. And Logan—the quietest of the three—touches something in me that feels far more dangerous than fear. They are the Astral Scions, sons of the Zodiac Council. And somehow, each of them looks at me like they're trying to solve a problem they can't escape. Aero elementals are meant to bind, anchor, and strengthen the other three elements—but the closer I get to them, the more their magic reacts to mine in ways no one at Astral Veil can explain. And worse? Part of me is starting to crave the feeling of it.

As breaches tear through the Harmony Barrier surrounding the academy, students start losing control of their elements in terrifying ways. Emotions bleed into magic. Shadows move where they shouldn't. Storms form inside classrooms. And beneath it all, whispers spread of the forgotten Thirteenth sign, erased from history itself. The professors insist Astral Veil remains safe, but the closer I get to whatever is happening to me, the more I realize something inside the academy has already begun to unravel.

And if I'm right, my awakening may not save Astral Veil.

It may be the thing that destroys it.

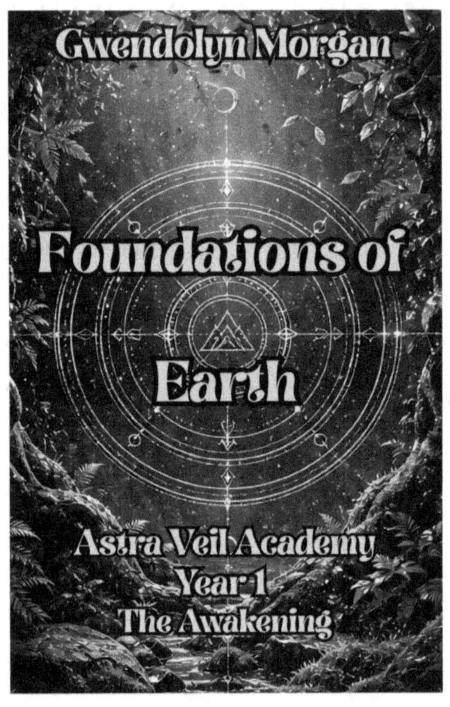

If you are interested in joining Gwendolyn's ARC Team or newsletter to get exclusive access to book releases, preview chapters, and all sorts of other goodies, visit her website and join today!

www.authorgwenmorgan.com

www.ingramcontent.com/pod-product-compliance
Lightning Source LLC
Chambersburg PA
CBHW070852160726
48004CB00003B/1048